MISSING
WITNESS

If a person who could have been a witness at the trial is not called by the State to testify, you may be able to infer that the person's testimony would have been unfavorable to the State.

State of Washington
Pattern Criminal Jury Instruction 5.20

CHAPTER 1

"At least he saw it coming."

Homicide D.A. Dave Brunelle considered his companion's comment as he stared down at the dead man under the Interstate-5 overpass. The fluorescent streetlights cast black the dried river of blood that had spilled out of the gunshot wound in the center of the dead man's forehead. Brunelle nodded toward the semiautomatic handgun lying on the pavement a few inches from the victim's right hand. "Too bad he didn't see it a few seconds sooner."

Seattle Police Detective Larry Chen shrugged his large shoulders. Brunelle was a tall man, mid-40s, with shortly cropped hair and a solid build, but still looked slight next to the beefy detective. "Then you'd be charging *him* with murder instead of the other guy," Chen said.

Brunelle smiled weakly at that. There was something to the criticism. The defense bar regularly accused the Prosecutor's Office of charging whoever won the fight. But when the loser ended up dead, there wasn't anyone else to charge.

"I can't charge anyone," Brunelle pointed out, "if you don't find that other guy. Any leads?"

It was shortly after 2:00 a.m. in Seattle's International District, formerly known as 'Chinatown,' just south of downtown and east of the stadiums. But even after the official name change, there was still an unmistakably Chinese-American feel to the area; even the street signs were in both English and Hànzi. Still, many of the newer store signs were in Japanese, Korean, or Vietnamese, with even a handful of foreign, but non-Asian, businesses peeking out between the noodle houses and import stores. Brunelle and Chen were standing in a large parking lot under the freeway and across the street from one of the district's most popular restaurants. Land was at a premium in the International District, like everywhere else in the Emerald City, but the only approved use for the space directly beneath the elevated freeway in earthquake-prone Seattle was a parking lot. It would be one thing if a section of expressway fell on a few dozen Subarus and Volvos; it would be quite another if it collapsed on a restaurant full of people enjoying hot pot or dim sum.

The lot was mostly empty, the only cars being the ones whose owners were unlucky enough to still be parked there when the police arrived and cordoned off the lot as an active crime scene. And a murder scene at that. Those surprised citizens who had returned to get their cars after a Saturday evening of dining and dancing were turned away and encouraged to take an Uber home, which was probably a good idea for most of them anyway, lest they get pulled over for a DUI as they drove by the half dozen police cars that clogged the intersection of South Jackson Street and 8th Avenue South.

Chen turned and pointed at the restaurant across 8th Avenue. "That's the reporting party," he indicated the man standing outside the front door, flanked by a couple of uniformed patrol officers. "Let's see what he has to say."

Brunelle agreed and the two men turned away from the shooting victim, although the dead man was anything but alone. Uniformed officers guarded the perimeter against curious interlopers, forensic techs were combing the scene for possible evidence to mark and photograph, and everyone was waiting for the Medical Examiner to arrive and begin the painstaking process of documenting and collecting the body. It would be at least half a day before the crime scene tape would finally come down and people could retrieve their cars. Good thing parking was free on Sundays.

"Mr. Han?" Chen greeted the man as they reached the entrance of the restaurant. Brunelle knew Chen had gotten his name from the dispatch log or another officer, probably both. The best detectives already knew the background when they spoke to someone; that way they could get right to what mattered most. "My name is Larry Chen. I'm the lead detective." He gestured toward his companion. "And this is Dave Brunelle. He's a prosecutor with the King County Prosecutor's Office. We'd like to ask you a few questions."

"Of course," Mr. Han replied. "Anything I can do to help. I've already told these officers what I saw."

Chen looked to the officer with the stripes on her arm. "Description?"

The sergeant nodded. "Vehicle, make and model, with a partial plate," she reported. "Suspect, height and weight, race and gender, age range."

"Good," Chen responded. He jerked a thumb back toward the parking lot. "Go see if Detective Montero needs any help back there."

The sergeant acknowledged the order and departed, the other two officers in tow. That left just Brunelle, Chen, and Mr. Han in the pool of light at the front door of the restaurant.

"What did you see?" Chen started as he pulled out a notebook to keep track of the witnesses' statements. "And when did you see it?"

"Actually, I heard something before I saw anything," Han replied. He was an older man, with gray at his temples, and dressed in the vest and pants of a three-piece suit. It was cool out, but there was no rain, and heat radiated off the building. "I was at the front of the restaurant, greeting customers. We get a rush around one o'clock, when people are looking for one last drink and maybe a bite to eat before heading home. We're mostly a restaurant, but we have a small bar area. At the end of the day, I like to greet people and figure out whether I should bother giving them a table. I don't want them taking up a table if they just want a drink. I'll make them wait a little until a spot opens up at the bar. I had just made it up front when I heard the shots."

"So, it was one a.m.?" Chen confirmed.

Han shrugged. "Probably a little after," he admitted. "I don't always rush to the front right at one. It just depends on how busy we are. Honestly, we weren't that busy tonight, so I wasn't in a hurry."

"How many shots did you hear?" Brunelle put in. He knew they needed to pin down the time of the shots, but that would be as easy as comparing the time of the 911 call with Han's answer to the question, 'How long did you wait from the time you heard the shots until you called the police?' which was almost certainly going to be, 'I called immediately' or something like that. Plus, there were likely additional calls from neighbors who heard the shots too. The time of the shots wouldn't really be in question. But the *number* of shots—that could make or break his case.

Han didn't hesitate. "Two. There were two shots."

"One right after another?" Brunelle followed up. "Or was there a pause between the two?"

Another important distinction. A long pause could indicate time taken to walk up to the victim after incapacitating him to deliver a kill shot.

"No pause," Han answered. "But not super-fast either. Not bang-bang. More like, bang," he waited one second, then, "bang."

Brunelle nodded. That could mean a lot of things, not all of them good. Maybe the victim did fire first, and the kill shot was return fire. They'd need to check that gun by his hand to see if it had been fired. Was there gunshot residue on his hand? Was there a discharged casing near his body? Did the marks on the casing match the gun's ejector pin? How many experts did it take to determine whether someone fired a gun? At least three, if there wasn't an eyewitness.

"You didn't see the person who fired the shots?" Brunelle just wanted to confirm he didn't have that eyewitness. Not yet, at least.

"No." Han shook his head. "But as soon as I heard the shots, I ran outside."

Not smart, Brunelle thought, *but helpful. Maybe.* "What did you see?"

"I saw a man running from the parking lot to a car parked right in front of the stop sign on Eighth Avenue." Han pointed to where 8th Avenue South joined South Jackson Street in a T-intersection, with motorists on two-lane 8th having to turn left or right onto the busier, five-lane Jackson. "You can't park in front of a stop sign," Han added.

"I'm aware of that," Chen replied. He squinted toward the intersection. "So that's about, what, a hundred feet?"

"Maybe two," Brunelle opined. "But less than a football field anyway."

That was good. Still too far for a credible in-court identification. If they did find the killer, Han wouldn't be able to come into court and say for sure it was him. Establishing the identity might take more experts, and probably a detective or two.

"Did you see a gun in his hand?" Brunelle asked anyway. Every little bit helped.

Han shrugged again. "I'm not sure. Maybe. It looked like he could have had something in his hand. But it was pretty far away, and it's pretty dark over there, even with the streetlights. I just know it was a young Asian man, tall and skinny, dressed in all black."

"But you didn't recognize him?" Chen tried.

Han shook his head. "No. Not from that distance anyway. Maybe I know him, but probably not. I didn't recognize the car either. White Camry, recent model."

"How did you get the plate?" Brunelle realized.

"I ran after him," Han answered.

Again, not smart, but helpful.

"But he pulled away before I could get the whole plate. I just got the first three letters."

"And you gave all of that information to my officers?" Chen confirmed.

"Of course," Han answered. "I want to help in any way I can. I grew up here. My father started this restaurant. I don't want this kind of violence in my neighborhood."

"No one does," Chen answered.

Brunelle glanced back at the crime scene tape. "Well, someone does," he observed. "But let's find out who it is and explain to him why he's wrong."

CHAPTER 2

Brunelle and Chen headed back to the parking lot to see if the Medical Examiner had made it there yet. It would take a full autopsy to extract all of the forensic information they needed from the dead man's remains, but there were usually some preliminary observations that could be helpful at this earliest of stages.

Then again, preliminary observations could be deceiving.

The M.E. was there all right, or more correctly, one of the several *Assistant* Medical Examiners employed by King County. Autopsies weren't just for murders, and there were over two million people in the county, 38.4 of whom died every day. One person couldn't possibly do all the things a large urban county needed from its medical examiner. So, there were several Assistant M.E.s, who, just like the county's several homicide prosecutors, were on call any given night in case someone took a bullet between the eyes under the freeway in Chinatown.

Brunelle just didn't think it would be her again so soon. Or, rather he'd hoped it wouldn't.

'Thinking' said it would happen, eventually.

'Hoping' said maybe it wouldn't, ever.

But as he and Chen ducked under the crime scene tape again and approached the victim, there she was, the Assistant M.E., crouched over the remains. Her thick black hair was a little longer, the curves under her jacket a little less curvy. But Brunelle was sure it was his ex-girlfriend, Kat Anderson, back from the dead—or the death of their relationship, anyway. The one he'd murdered.

Ah, irony.

But irony wasn't going to change the fact that it was Brunelle's case, and Brunelle was going to have to prosecute it, scorned ex-girlfriend or not. As they reached her, Chen seemed oblivious to the imminent disaster. Brunelle couldn't think of anything else.

What do you say to a woman who has every reason to hate you and probably does, but you have to talk to her anyway? In a dark parking lot? Over a dead body?

If you're like most men, you make a joke, of course.

"Hey, there," his voice broke from behind her. "What's a pretty girl like you doing over a dead body like this?"

Chen turned and frowned at him, but it was nothing compared to the expression of the woman he'd just called a 'pretty girl.' The woman looked back over her shoulder at Brunelle, confirming that she was most definitely not Kat Anderson, and was even more definitely incensed at Brunelle's opening comment.

"What did you say to me?" she asked as she stood up from her examination of the body.

She was several inches taller than Kat, almost as tall as Brunelle himself, in fact. She was older than Kat, too, in her 50s, with small glasses and a sharp nose. There was also an unmistakable glint of anger in her eyes— which didn't make her not look like Kat, but was nevertheless the most noticeable feature of her expression just then.

"Uh…" Brunelle started, as his brain tried to reconcile his relief that he wasn't confronted with his ex-girlfriend with his embarrassment at having made that comment to someone he didn't even know. "I, I'm sorry. I thought you were someone else."

"A pretty girl?" the M.E. crossed her arms.

"Uh, yes," Brunelle replied at first, his brain too occupied to do anything but answer simply and truthfully. But then he finally caught himself. "I mean, no. I thought you were someone I haven't seen in a while. A friend. Well, she used to be." He shrugged. "Just someone I used to know."

The Assistant Medical Examiner didn't uncross her arms. "Uh-huh," she said dubiously.

Mercifully, Chen finally stepped in. With another frown at Brunelle, he introduced them. "Dave, this is Dr. Marianne Delacourt. She's the newest Assistant Medical Examiner for the county. She came over from Spokane County last month. Doctor, this is Dave Brunelle, one of the county's homicide prosecutors. It's his night to be on call."

"Hi." Brunelle stuck out a hand, eager to get past the situation he'd caused. "Nice to meet you."

But Delacourt seemed less willing to move on. She didn't take Brunelle's hand. "I wish I could say the same."

Brunelle pulled his hand back and cast his glance to the side.

Delacourt turned hers to Chen. "There are at least two gunshot wounds," she reported. "The obvious one to the forehead, and another to the anterior torso. I expect it's an entrance wound but I won't know for sure until the autopsy. And I can't foreclose the possibility of discovering more injuries once I get his clothes off."

Brunelle knew damn well not to make any jokes about that. "The witness said there were two shots."

Delacourt offered a smirk. "I don't care what the witness said," she declared. "I'm a scientist. Witnesses don't enter into it at all."

"Well, they do for me," Brunelle defended. "I'm a lawyer."

"Again," Delacourt blinked at him, "I don't care."

Brunelle stifled a sigh. Maybe it would have been better if it had been Kat. But yeah, no, probably not.

"Chen!" It was Detective Julia Montero, with her usual leather jacket and long black ponytail. Chen was the lead detective, but murder scenes were all-hands-on-deck. There were at least four detectives there. Montero was waving over at them, a cell phone pressed to her ear. "They found the car. It's straight up Jackson at Seventeenth. Perp is holed up in his apartment. S.W.A.T. is on their way."

"Great!" Brunelle seized the opportunity to depart the company of Dr. Marianne Delacourt. He clapped Chen on the shoulder and started toward their cars. "Let's go."

CHAPTER 3

It may have been only nine blocks to the apartment of the suspected shooter, but they were all uphill, and a pretty steep hill at that. There was no way Brunelle was going to walk that far. Not when time was of the essence. Although probably not at all, if he was honest with himself. He was in decent enough shape for a man in his mid-to-late 40s, but he knew he didn't deserve any credit for it. It was genetics, not dedication to physical fitness. He came from a long line of naturally thin men who worked desk jobs, but could still eat dessert without worrying too much about their waistlines. Of course, most of them also died early of heart disease.

Brunelle rode shotgun in Chen's unmarked car, which gave the detective the chance to ask his friend, once the car doors were closed, "What the hell was that?"

"I thought she was Kat," Brunelle defended. "I got nervous."

"Kat?" Chen laughed, but darkly. "Oh, wow. That would have been even worse. 'Pretty girl'? Kat would have ripped your throat out with her own nails."

Brunelle nodded. "Yeah, you're probably right."

Chen activated the vehicle's hidden emergency lights and blew through the traffic lights at 12th Avenue South and Rainier Avenue South.

"Don't worry," Chen told him as they approached the neighborhood where the suspect vehicle was located. It was dominated by an enormous red neon 'WONDER BREAD' sign that had been saved by the Seattle Historical Society and therefore still stood atop the condo complex the old bread factory had been converted into years before. Seattle was a weird city sometimes. "Kat took a job in California. That's why there was an opening for Dr. Delacourt." He pulled the car over behind the row of marked patrol cars, their own emergency equipment flashing, that had coalesced in front of the suspect's apartment complex. "I thought you knew that."

Brunelle frowned. He shook his head. "No, she didn't tell me. We didn't really talk, you know, after we... Well, I..." but he didn't finish the sentence.

He didn't have to. Chen knew the story. "Yeah. That makes sense." He turned off the car and opened his door. "Come on. Let's get the sit rep."

The situation seemed pretty obvious to Brunelle. There were a dozen cop cars in the immediate area, several of them blocking traffic in both directions on Jackson in front of the suspect's apartment, a squat two-story affair, with a neon '24-Hour Massage' blinking lewdly in one of the downstairs windows. A Seattle P.D. S.W.A.T. van was parked strategically near the entrance to the apartments, with officers in full body armor huddled behind it, awaiting orders. Brunelle knew there was also a sniper stationed somewhere nearby, maybe up by that glaring 'WONDER BREAD' sign.

He hung back while Chen did his cop thing. It was good for a prosecutor to get called out to a murder scene—even in the middle of the night—so any potential evidence problems could be identified and neutralized in the moment. But the King County Prosecutor's Office didn't hand out body armor. Desperate murderers holed up in their apartments— that was cop stuff, not lawyer stuff. He could make sure they Mirandized him *after* he was safely in handcuffs.

Chen returned to brief Brunelle, who had made his way to the back of the car, placing the vehicle between him and whatever window of the worn, two-story apartment building he was likely to get shot at from.

"It's definitely him," Chen informed him. "Neighbors confirmed his identity. Jeremy Nguyen, twenty-three, five-foot ten, hundred and sixty pounds, drives a white Camry, which we found a half block up the street."

"Sounds like we got our man," Brunelle replied. "Try not to kill him, or I won't have anything to do."

Chen laughed and nodded toward the apartment building. "Tell *him* that. He'll be fine if he gives himself up. But he so much as raises a hand like he's got a gun in it, and he'll be dead before he hits the pavement."

Brunelle knew that was true. And there'd be no questioning the officers' actions. Washington had several statutes about lawful use of force and justifiable homicide. In addition to the standard self-defense statute that applied to regular citizens, there was a special one just for law enforcement officers attempting to effectuate an arrest. All justifiable homicides were legal, but some were more legal than others.

"S.W.A.T. has a hostage negotiator who's trying to get Nguyen on the line," Chen continued. "If all goes well—"

But the rest of his sentence was drowned out by the shouted orders of a dozen cops, weapons leveled at the tall, thin, young Asian man who had just walked out of the apartment building, his arms raised high and wide. Chen drew his own pistol and leveled it at the suspect over the hood of his vehicle.

Brunelle—suddenly very aware of both the overwhelming amount of firepower being aimed from multiple directions at someone uncomfortably close to him, and his own lack of any such firepower—decided to lower himself behind the car as well. It was pretty clear to him that Jeremy Nguyen wasn't armed, but all it took was one nervous rookie cop to ignite an explosion of gunfire.

"On your knees! Now!" shouted one of the S.W.A.T. officers. "Hands on your head! Now! Do it!"

From what Brunelle could see through the vehicle windows, Nguyen was complying with all commands. That didn't keep the cops from ensuring his compliance with some rather forceful hands-on encouragement. The kind that would probably show up in the booking photo.

Then again, Brunelle thought, *don't murder someone and flee the scene with the gun.* He felt pretty confident the jury would understand a couple of scrapes and bruises.

In less time than it took to say, 'You have the right to remain silent,' Nguyen was handcuffed and secured in the back of one of the patrol cars. The reason it took less time than that was because none of the cops bothered to say it. There would be time for that later.

Figuring the situation was under control, Brunelle stood up again, groaning at the way his knees popped. "You gonna interrogate him now?"

"Damn right," Chen answered, also standing, but seemingly energized by the confrontation. "You wanna watch?"

Brunelle rubbed his right knee, the pain lingering a bit longer each time he forgot he wasn't young enough to crouch down behind cars any more. "Damn right."

CHAPTER 4

The closest precinct to the arrest location was the main S.P.D. headquarters downtown. That worked well for Chen because his office was located there, along with his assigned parking spot in the underground garage. Detectives didn't usually do transports, except maybe of tag-along prosecutors, and security always slowed things down, so Brunelle and Chen had a few minutes to wait at the station before the two transport officers arrived with Nguyen. They took him directly to one of the interrogation rooms and handcuffed him to the suspect chair, lest he get any ideas of trying to resist or flee. But from what Brunelle had observed, Nguyen had been nothing but compliant.

"Make sure to read him his rights," Brunelle reminded Chen before the detective went in to talk with Nguyen.

Chen raised an eyebrow. "That's your advice? Gee, thanks. Should I also not hit him?"

Brunelle nodded thoughtfully. "Yes, I would advise not brutalizing the suspect. It may call into question the voluntariness of his confession."

"Hey, thanks, counselor." Det. Montero slapped Brunelle's back as she came up from behind him. "I left my rubber hoses in my other car anyway."

"Anything else we should keep in mind?" Chen asked, only half-jokingly. He understood Brunelle's role in ultimately holding the killer responsible. If there might be something special the prosecutor needed to get that guilty verdict, it was worth asking.

But Brunelle shook his head. "No. Just the basics. Who, what, where, and why."

"Not when?" Montero teased. "Or how?"

Brunelle thought for a moment. "We already know when. But sure, how is always good. Just in case there's more to it than our scientist medical examiner is able to determine from the autopsy alone."

Montero noticed the edge in Brunelle's voice and looked to Chen for an explanation.

"I'll tell you later," he offered. "It's pretty funny actually."

Brunelle wasn't sure that was true, but it wasn't the time to argue the point. It was time to interrogate a murder suspect.

"What do we know about him?" Brunelle asked, nodding toward the interrogation room. "Any history?"

"Yeah, but nothing violent," Chen reported. "Drugs mostly. He started with simple possession, then graduated to a possession with intent to deliver. Looks like he was trying to graduate from user to seller. But nothing violent like this."

"Maybe drug dealing lost its thrill," Brunelle posited. "He's ready for the big leagues."

"Hell of a way to graduate to the big leagues." Chen shook his head. "Let's see if he can explain why such a big jump."

Brunelle stepped into the observation room to watch through the two-way mirror as Chen and Montero entered the interrogation room and engaged their subject.

Nguyen didn't look scared exactly, but he did seem nervous. In that way, he seemed intelligent. He should be nervous. He was handcuffed to a chair with two experienced police detectives about to interrogate him about a murder he'd committed that very night. The body probably wasn't even cold yet.

"Jeremy," Chen started in a friendly tone. "My name is Larry Chen. This is Julia Montero. We're detectives, and we'd like to talk to you a little bit about what happened tonight."

It might have seemed like Chen was going to be the good cop to Montero's bad cop, but it was Seattle. They were both going to be good cops.

Nguyen didn't reply. He just eyed the detectives for several seconds. Finally, he gave a small nod.

"Good, good," Chen said in reply to the nod. "Now, we just need to make sure you know your rights, okay? First of all, you have the right to remain silent. Second, you have the right to speak with an attorney before answering any questions. If you can't afford an attorney, one will be provided to you at public expense…"

Chen went on. There were a few more variations on the theme to go through before the real questions started.

"Do you understand each of these rights?" Chen asked at the end of the rights, his tone like that of a friendly school guidance counselor. The cool one.

Nguyen nodded. "Yes."

"And having these rights in mind," Chen concluded with the payoff question, "do you wish to speak with us about what happened tonight?"

Nguyen's brow furrowed. He looked back and forth between the detectives, then around the room, as if there might be someone else there to help him answer the question.

"Jeremy?" Chen prodded. "Are you willing to talk with us? We want to hear your side of the story."

Nguyen stopped glancing around the room. He stared at Chen for what became an uncomfortably long time. He looked quickly at Montero, then back at Chen. Finally, he started nodding very fast, then stopped, exhaled, and announced, "Self-defense."

"Fuck," Brunelle hissed as he threw up his hands.

Chen blinked at Nguyen for a moment. "Self-defense?" he echoed.

"Yes." Nguyen nodded. "Self-defense."

Chen waited for more, but Nguyen didn't say anything else. "What does that mean exactly?" Chen prodded. "You were acting in self-defense?"

Nguyen nodded again, but didn't answer.

"Tell us what that means," Montero encouraged. "What happened? Why did you have to defend yourself?"

Brunelle stood behind the observation glass, his arms crossed tightly across his chest. Asserting self-defense wasn't actually the worst thing Nguyen could have said. Acting in self-defense was at least an admission of acting in the first place. It wouldn't be an ID case. Nguyen wouldn't claim alibi and wheel in an elderly grandmother to say he was with her all night. Generally speaking, there were only two ways to defend a murder charge: 'I didn't do it,' or 'I had to do it.' Nguyen was choosing Option B.

The real problem with a self-defense claim was that a defendant didn't have to prove it—the prosecution had to *disprove* it, and disprove it beyond a reasonable doubt. That could be difficult when the only witnesses to the crime were the defendant and the dead man.

Chen and Montero needed to get Nguyen talking. It was one thing to just assert 'self-defense.' It was another to make it believable. You can't just shoot someone because you were scared, or they looked at you wrong, or you thought they were going to beat you up. You can't bring a gun to a fist fight. The devil was in the details, as they say, and self-defense was in the facts. It had only been a few hours since the murder. Between firing the shots, fleeing the scene, and surrendering to the police, Nguyen probably hadn't had the opportunity to come up with an internally consistent, externally believable story to support his self-defense claim. He'd be stuck with whatever he told Chen and Montero right then. The only thing that could get in the way of that was if Nguyen lawyered up.

"Mr. Brunelle," a uniformed officer opened the door to the observation room. "I wasn't sure who to tell, but there's an attorney at the front desk. He's claiming he represents the murder suspect and is demanding to see him."

Double fuck, Brunelle thought.

He sighed. "Who is it?"

The officer thought for a moment. "He said his name is Welles. William Harrison Welles."

And triple fuck.

* * *

"David!" Welles enthused as Brunelle entered the police station lobby, the patrol officer hanging back to wait at the secure entry. Even at that hour, he was dressed in a suit that cost more than Brunelle's monthly salary, his gray ponytail resting on the back of the perfectly tailored collar. "So good to see you again. Now I *know* my client is back there. You wouldn't be here at this hour unless there was some poor citizen being worked over by the Boys in Blue."

William Harrison Welles was one of the more noteworthy members of Seattle's defense bar. Not because he was necessarily that good, but because he made sure people took note of him. He was on a first name basis with every news reporter in Seattle.

"No cameras?" Brunelle gestured vaguely behind Welles. "I didn't know you travelled without them."

Welles smirked even as he shook Brunelle's outstretched hand. "There will be plenty of time for that, old friend. But for now, I'd like to speak with my client, please."

Brunelle crossed his arms. "Yeah, about that. No one here has mentioned having you as their attorney. That would be the sort of thing I'd notice."

"Yes, well, not everyone is as well versed in the law as you and I," Welles replied. "Hence our occupations. But I can assure you, I represent Jeremy Nguyen, and we both know he is here being questioned by police—now in violation of his right to counsel."

But Brunelle shook his head. "*He* has to assert that right, not you. There's case law on that."

"Case law regarding suppression of his confession perhaps," Welles conceded. "But what about case law regarding prosecutorial misconduct? I can get an entire case thrown out for that."

Brunelle frowned. "I haven't spoken with Nguyen. That's not my job."

"Of course it's not," Welles agreed. "My heavens, no. A prosecutor conducting an interrogation? That would be ludicrous. Who would you call as a witness as to what the defendant said? No, no. I just mean, you now know that I represent Mr. Nguyen. Under the Rules of Professional Conduct, any communications with a represented person must go through that person's attorney. And there's plenty of case law about how the police and prosecutors are both agents of the same state. Do you really want to explain to the Bar Association that you denied me access to my client because it was your cops talking to him and not you personally?"

"How do I know for sure that you actually represent him?" Brunelle asked.

Welles's eyes widened. "Why, David. Because I told you so."

Brunelle thought about that for a moment. Then he relented. In fact, he'd already told Chen to pause the interrogation while he spoke with Welles. There was a chance Welles had just heard about the shooting and was sniffing around for press. But Welles knew Nguyen's name, a detail that hadn't been released yet. That meant someone had hired him. Not Nguyen himself, or else he would have asked for Welles rather than agreeing to talk, or sort of talk, to detectives. More likely it was Nguyen's parents, desperate to help their son, and remembering Welles's name from some news report they'd seen last summer.

"Fine," Brunelle exhaled. "You can talk with your guy. It's not like he said much anyway."

"What did he say?" Welles asked as Brunelle turned them toward the door where the officer was waiting.

"The only thing he said," Brunelle answered, "was 'self-defense.'"

"Really?" Welles smiled broadly. "Oh yes, I can work with that."

CHAPTER 5

As little as Brunelle had wanted to see Welles in the police station lobby, it was nothing compared to how much less he wanted to see Madame Delacourt at the autopsy. But the good doctor had been right—the information from the post-mortem examination would be uncontaminated by the biases and limits of eyewitness testimony. And that was likely to make it the most persuasive evidence in the entire case. Too bad she was the witness he would have to call to the stand to get that evidence admitted. When presenting that important of evidence, it was always better if the jury liked the witness. Brunelle was sure they wouldn't like Marianne Delacourt.

Well, at least, he didn't like her.

But only because she didn't seem to like him.

Brunelle shook his head sharply. He was sitting in the lobby of the King County Medical Examiner's Office. Chen was sitting next to him, half-reading a months-old copy of *Sports Illustrated*. It was a little after eight o'clock in the morning. The office was still closed to the general public, but Brunelle and Chen weren't the general public. They were lead cop and lead prosecutor on a murder case. Delacourt started her day at eight and her first autopsy would be their victim from beneath the overpass. They'd come to observe, and, if necessary, advise. Brunelle took a deep breath and told himself to give Delacourt a second chance. It had been the middle of the night, and he had said something stupid. But that was in the past. She was probably a very nice person who would be happy to see them both, to make sure she did as thorough a job as necessary to help hold the man's killer responsible.

Or not.

"What is he doing here?" Delacourt demanded as soon as she came out to the lobby to greet them. Or to greet Chen, anyway. She pointed at Brunelle, but addressed her question squarely to the detective.

"Homicide prosecutors regularly attend the autopsies, doctor," Chen started.

Brunelle finished for him. He didn't need a speaking agent. "I'm here to observe and ask questions. The shooter is claiming self-defense. I want to see if there's any evidence of that."

"I'm not going to give an opinion about self-defense," Delacourt answered. "That's a legal concept about blame and justification. I don't care about any of that."

"You don't care if that man was murdered?" Brunelle challenged.

Delacourt thought for a moment. "No," she said. "I don't. Not professionally anyway. Murder is a legal definition, an unjustified killing. I only care if it was homicide, not murder. Or manslaughter. Or self-defense."

"All the more reason I should be here," Brunelle remarked.

"All the more reason you shouldn't," Delacourt returned. "This is a medical procedure, a scientific inquiry. Not some legal circus act, trying to fit the world into societal definitions of right and wrong that change and morph with every generation."

"I'm pretty sure murder has been in the 'wrong' column for a while now," Brunelle said. "Ten Commandments and all that."

Delacourt scoffed. "Don't even start with the contamination of religious doctrine into our jurisprudence. If I hear—"

"Doctor," Chen interrupted. "I think Dave is just trying to say he might have some questions, and it will be easier to ask you during the procedure than afterward when it might be too late to find the answer."

Delacourt took a moment, her expression hardening, before answering, "My examination will be as complete and thorough as it always is, regardless of whether some lawyer doesn't understand what I'm doing. I'm the one who went to medical school."

"And I went to law school," Brunelle put in.

But Delacourt scoffed. "Oh, please. Law school was for the kids who didn't have the stomach for medical school or the drive for business school."

"Wow," Brunelle said. "Look, I'm sorry if I offended you last night. I mistook you for someone else who would have understood that what I said was a joke. But either way, we need to put that behind us. A man was killed last night, murdered, and the man who killed him is sitting in the King County Jail awaiting charges. He claimed self-defense last night, but didn't give any details. So, I need to get the details from you. I need to know if it was self-defense, and if it wasn't, I need to be able to prove that. I need to know if there was gunshot residue on his hands so I know whether he fired his own gun. I need to know if there was burning or stippling at the gunshot wounds so I know whether the killer's gun was within eighteen inches or it was a shot across the parking lot. I need to know if there were any other injuries that might suggest a struggle, especially wounds to the hand that might mean a struggle for the murder weapon. Those are the types of things I need to know. That's why I'm here."

"I won't testify to any of that," Delacourt snapped back. "I'm a pathologist, not a crime scene reconstructionist."

"You won't testify whether there was stippling around the gunshot wounds?" Brunelle asked.

"Whether there is or there isn't, I won't testify that it means anything one way or the other," Delacourt said. "I will testify as to what the injuries were and what mechanism caused them, but I will not speculate as to how or why they were inflicted."

Brunelle blinked at her. "I need someone who will explain to the jury the significance of no stippling at the site of the gunshot wounds."

"I can tell you whether any such stippling is present," Delacourt said, "but I will not tell you what that means in regard to how far away the firearm was. I'm not a ballistics expert."

Brunelle thought for a moment. "Don't you use that sort of evidence to determine the cause of death? If it's a contact wound, it might be suicide, right?"

"If it's a sealed wound, it's almost certainly suicide," Delacourt answered. "If it's a contact wound, the person might have pulled away slightly as the slayer pulled the trigger."

Brunelle pointed both hands at her. "See? That. That's the kind of thing I need explained to a jury."

But Delacourt shook her head. "I said 'might' and I won't testify to 'mights'."

Brunelle crossed his arms. "Then maybe someone else should do this autopsy."

Delacourt's eyes flared. "Are you challenging my professional capabilities?"

"I'm challenging your understanding of them," Brunelle replied. "You aren't some private pathologist who got hired by the family because they think the old folks home mixed up grandpa's medications. You work for the county, just like me. And when someone gets rolled into your freezer with a bullet between his eyes, you damn well better be ready to come into court and tell the jury why."

Delacourt tilted her head slightly and stared at Brunelle, her eyes still wide—and angry. After several seconds, she shook that same head. "No." She pointed at Brunelle again, but again addressed Chen. "He can't come back. He can't observe the autopsy."

"What?" Brunelle let out. "You've got to be kid—"

Chen put a hand up to silence his friend. "I'd like him present," he told the doctor. "He may put his foot in his mouth more often than a baby learning to roll over, but he's experienced, and he knows what he needs— what *we* need—for this case."

Brunelle opened his palms at Chen. *A baby learning to roll over?* But he didn't say anything.

Delacourt did, though. "No. Absolutely not. It's my autopsy, my examination room, my decision. This man will not be present. End of discussion."

They could call in a different prosecutor, but then Brunelle would lose the case to that person. And he wasn't giving up the case.

"Give me a moment," Chen told the doctor, then pulled Brunelle aside. "You need to go."

Brunelle threw those hands wide again. "Are you shitting me? This is my case."

"And if you want it to stay that way, you'll leave," Chen answered. "I don't know why she hates you—well, okay, maybe I can see why, but—"

"What?" Brunelle interjected.

"But," Chen pressed on, "she does. And we both want her to do her best job on this one. That might not happen if you're nearby, aggravating her."

"I'm not aggravating," Brunelle protested.

Chen shrugged and smiled slightly. "You can be aggravating sometimes," he joked. "But right now needs to not be one of those times. She needs to do a top-rate job—which she will—and then it'll be your turn to do a top-notch job—which you will."

Brunelle frowned, but didn't immediately push back.

Chen knew what that meant and pressed his advantage. "I know what needs to be in the autopsy report," he assured him. "I know about gunshot residue, and stippling, and defensive wounds, and all that. I'll make sure everything gets in there. You go to your office and start drafting up the charging documents. I'll come straight over after the autopsy and let you know what she found."

"And didn't find," Brunelle reminded him.

"And didn't find, right," Chen agreed. "I'll come straight over."

Brunelle sighed. "You better. I can't charge somebody with murder if the autopsy shows self-defense."

Chen shook his head. "It's not going to show self-defense."

"I know," Brunelle replied.

"It's agreed then," Chen concluded. "I'll check in with you in a couple of hours. Now, get out of here before that corpse starts rotting."

Brunelle glared over at Delacourt. "You mean her?"

"Now, now, David," Chen chided him. "Be nice. You're going to need her at the trial, whether she likes it or not."

Brunelle frowned. "I hope she doesn't like it."

Chen patted him on the shoulder. "That's the spirit. Now, shoo. I have work to do, and so do you."

* * *

Brunelle spent the morning preparing charging documents for two different crimes: murder in the first degree or murder in the second degree. Murder Two meant intentional killing; Murder One meant both intentional and premeditated. But premeditated needed a reason—something more than two guys meeting on the street and deciding to have a shoot-out. The shot to the victim's forehead was clearly intended to kill, but Brunelle would need a motive to prove premeditation. The suspect's two-word claim of 'self-defense' didn't give him that motive. And the dead man wasn't going to tell them either.

Or then again, maybe he would. After a fashion.

Chen arrived just as Brunelle had resigned himself to charging Murder in the Second Degree, its penalties roughly half that of Murder One. But at the sight of the detective, Brunelle moved his cursor off the 'PRINT' button and looked up expectantly. "Well?"

Chen shrugged. "Mostly, the autopsy showed what we expected," he reported. "No stippling of the wounds, or even the clothing around the wounds, so the shot was from a distance. No defensive wounds to the hands or arms, so there was no struggle. No gunshot residue on his hands, so he didn't fire his own gun."

Brunelle nodded and looked again at his computer screen. That was all good news. But it wasn't quite enough to get them to premeditation. Then his brain reminded him of the word Chen had started with. He turned back to the detective. "Mostly?"

Chen grinned. "Well, there was nothing else forensically. I mean, it was a hell of a shot, right between the eyes, from at least a few feet away. But, medically speaking, the cut-and-gut didn't uncover any mysteries."

"So what did?" Brunelle suspected he was supposed to ask.

Chen's smile broadened and he produced a clear evidence bag from behind his back. "The inventory search of our dead man's clothes. This was in his inside jacket pocket."

Brunelle took the baggie. It was already sealed with red evidence tape, signed and dated by Chen himself. As long as Brunelle didn't break the seal, the chain of custody wouldn't be impacted by his examining it. In fact, that was exactly why it was in a clear baggie: so that he, and eventually Welles, and finally the jury, could look through the plastic at what was inside. And what was inside was a note with a name and partial number scrawled on it:

J O A N   I N H A

2 0 6 -

"Who do you suppose Joan Inha is?" Brunelle mused aloud. Then, he waved away his own question. "Never mind. I don't need to know who she is. I know *what* she is."

"What is she?" Chen asked.

"She's the motive," Brunelle answered. "Nothing says premeditation like a love triangle and a shot between the eyes."

CHAPTER 6

"Murder One?" Welles frowned as he accepted the charging documents from Brunelle outside the arraignment courtroom. "Really, David? You think you can prove premeditation? You won't even be able to disprove self-defense. This is a manslaughter case at best. And most likely a straight acquittal."

Brunelle just shrugged and kept his confident smile. "You keep telling yourself that. And I'll tell the jury the classic tale of a love affair gone wrong, betrayal and jealousy, and a heartbroken man driven to murder."

Welles raised a bemused eyebrow. "What are you talking about?"

Brunelle nodded at the paperwork he'd given the defense attorney. "Read the declaration for probable cause. It's all in there, including the name of the woman they were fighting over."

Welles took several moments to skim the factual summary attached to the charging papers. "Joan Inha?" he asked finally. "Have you even talked to this woman? She could be the dead man's dry cleaner for all we know."

"You don't try to get the phone number of your dry cleaner," Brunelle responded. "The victim was clearly trying to get her name and number. Your guy got wind of it and decided to take matters into his own hands. Oldest story in the book."

"I'm not sure what books you're reading," Welles scoffed, "but they're clearly fiction. Fairy tales, even. This is the wildest of speculation."

Brunelle nodded. "Right now, maybe. But even as we speak, Detective Chen is tracking down Ms. Inha. I expect to have a formal witness statement to you by the end of the week. Even if she didn't see the murder, I bet she can establish the connection between your guy and the dead man."

Welles scoffed. "The connection is that the alleged victim threatened my client's life, and my client responded with lawful force."

Brunelle smirked, but before he could respond, Welles added, "And you can't prove otherwise. Certainly not beyond a reasonable doubt."

The smirk faded. "We'll see," Brunelle replied. "But for today, I don't have to. I just have to have probable cause to charge your guy, and I've got more than enough for that."

It was Welles's turn to smirk. "We'll see," he echoed.

The daily arraignment courtroom was a lot different from a trial courtroom. During a trial, one case is assigned to one courtroom in front of one judge, with one defendant, one defense attorney and one prosecutor. But the vast majority of criminal cases—over 90 percent—settled; they never saw the inside of a trial courtroom. But every one of those criminal cases, whether they were the 90 percent that settled or the ten percent that didn't, started with an arraignment. That meant an overcrowded courtroom, filled with prosecutors, public defenders, in-custody defendants in the back with corrections officers, and out-of-custody defendants in the gallery with friends and family. But there was still only one judge, and it was their job to bring order to the apparent chaos, and to do so before the lunch break because there was a full daily docket of pleas scheduled to start right at 1:00.

Day after day of nothing but arraignments and pleas wasn't a terribly desirable assignment for a judge, which is why it often went to one of the newer judges. That day, for better or worse, it was Judge Karen Daniels, and she took the bench promptly at 9:00.

"All rise!" the bailiff announced the entrance of the judge. "The King County Superior Court is now in session, The Honorable Karen Daniels presiding."

Daniels had been a long-time public defender, trying some of the biggest cases in the county. When one of the older judges finally retired and a spot opened up, the Governor surprised everyone by appointing someone with integrity and experience, rather than just a partner at whatever corporate firm had donated the most to the campaign. So, the good news was, the arraignment would take place in front of a judge who truly understood criminal law. The bad news was, black robe or not, she was still a public defender at heart.

Judge Daniels settled into her seat above the fray. Her jaw-length black hair was the exact same shade as that black robe and the plastic frames of the glasses that rested at the end of her nose. "Are any matters ready?" she inquired.

Like most homicide prosecutors, Brunelle handled his own arraignments, but the majority of cases didn't actually need that level of personal attention at the arraignment. Those could be handled by a younger prosecutor who, like the judge and the public defender on the other end of the bar, was assigned to the arraignment rotation for a set amount of time before completing the transition from misdemeanor work in the District Court to finally getting assigned to a felony trial team and getting to cut their teeth on low level felonies like drug possession and car thefts. Judge Daniels's question was directed to the assigned prosecutor, a thin young man in a blue pinstripe suit standing directly in front of her, who acted as a sort of *maître d'* for the courtroom. Brunelle didn't know his name but had seen him around the office.

Jim something, maybe?

Upon hearing the judge's question, Jim—or whatever his name was—turned and looked to Brunelle to see if he was ready. He knew who Brunelle was. And if a homicide prosecutor was waiting to do an arraignment, he wasn't supposed to wait long. Brunelle confirmed he was ready with a sharp nod, and Jim informed the judge, "I believe Mr. Brunelle has a matter ready, Your Honor."

Daniels raised her gaze to Brunelle and Welles as they approached the bar and nodded to them both.

"Nguyen," Brunelle called out to the corrections officer next to the secure door to the holding cells, then took his place before the judge. Welles supplanted the assigned public defender—a young woman in a black pantsuit—and awaited the arrival of his client. A few moments later, Jeremy Nguyen, in orange jail garb and belly chains, stood next to his attorney and the arraignment could begin.

"Your Honor," Brunelle began, "this is the matter of the State of Washington versus Jeremy Huy Nguyen. It is on for arraignment this morning on one count of murder in the first degree. I am handing forward the information and declaration for determination of probable cause, copies of which have already been provided to the defense."

'Information' was the technical term for a felony complaint. In addition to being a little weird, Washington State was also very polite. Prosecutors didn't 'complain' about crimes, they simply 'informed' defendants that they were accused of committing them.

The bailiff accepted the papers from Brunelle and passed them up to the judge. Daniels took a few moments to review the documents, then proceeded.

"Mr. Welles, good morning," she began. "Have you received copies of the information and probable cause declaration?"

Welles nodded graciously, almost exaggeratedly. "Good morning, Your Honor. May it please the Court, William Harrison Welles on behalf of the accused, Mr. Jeremy Nguyen. We have received copies of the charging papers. We would waive further formal reading and enter a vehement plea of absolutely not guilty."

Brunelle nodded but didn't look up from the contemporaneous file notes he was taking. Most lawyers saved the theatrics just for when jurors were in the room. Not Welles. For him, all the world was a stage.

But it didn't matter. Arraignments were necessary, but there wasn't much drama. The State filed charges. The defendant pled not guilty. Then came the interesting part, arguing over bail. Brunelle figured he'd ask for a million, standard on murder cases; Welles would ask for a personal recognizance release; and Daniels would split the baby with a $500K bail. So, really, even that part was almost predictable. But no showman likes to be predictable.

"We *would* waive a formal reading and enter a plea of not guilty, Your Honor," Welles repeated, "*if* that were legally required. However, we instead move to strike the State's information as insufficient on its face and ask for the immediate and unconditional release of Mr. Nguyen until and unless the State is able to file charging paperwork that actually charges Mr. Nguyen with a cognizable offense under Washington law."

While Brunelle and Welles were at the bar, the courtroom behind them was still full of activity, from lawyers discussing their cases to corrections officers half-whispering into their shoulder-mounted radios. None of them had really been paying attention to what was happening on another lawyer's case. Until then.

The room went silent as the judge cocked her head at Welles. "I'm sorry, counsel," she said. "The defendant is charged with murder in the first degree, is he not?"

"I would argue that he is not, Your Honor, no," Welles replied. He pointed to the information still in the judge's hands. "At least by that document. It is facially deficient and, therefore, I submit facially invalid."

Brunelle looked down at his copy of the information. Had he forgotten something? They used a template for each crime, so the language wasn't novel. It named the crime and listed out the elements of the offense in exactly the same way as every other Murder One case his office filed. The only things that changed were the offense date and the victim's name. He confirmed it held all the standard language. It wasn't like murder was a complicated crime to define: 'A person is guilty of murder in the first degree when, with a premeditated intent to cause the death of another person, he or she causes the death of such person or of a third person.' RCW 9A.32.030(1)(a). And every word of it was in the information. He was stumped.

So, when Judge Daniels looked to him for some guidance, Brunelle told her as much. "I'm not sure what Mr. Welles is referring to, Your Honor. The information charges Mr. Nguyen with one count of murder in the first degree and lists all the statutory elements of that offense. The State believes the information is sufficient and would ask the Court to proceed with the arraignment, defense counsel's objection notwithstanding."

Daniels nodded along with Brunelle. She may have been a public defender, but that meant she knew what was supposed to be in an information. And the one against Nguyen sure seemed adequate.

"Mr. Welles," she returned her attention to the defense side of the bar, "perhaps you could explain more fully why you don't believe the information is sufficient to initiate criminal proceedings against your client. I agree with Mr. Brunelle. The information seems sufficient to me. It lists the names of the defendant and the alleged victim, the date of the offense, and the statutory elements of the crime. What's missing?"

Welles could tell everyone had stopped talking and was looking at him. And Brunelle could tell he loved it. "Ah, but does it, Your Honor? Does it truly list all the statutory elements which the State will be required to prove beyond a reasonable doubt? And if it does not charge those statutorily required elements, then how can the Court find that it is sufficient, constitutionally, to put my client on notice of the charges against him?"

When Daniels just raised an eyebrow at him, he added, "I would remind the Court that RCW 9A.32.030 is not the only statute that governs what the prosecution must prove in a murder case."

Brunelle finally understood. "Self-defense," he murmured.

"Yes!" Welles bellowed, with a gesture toward his opponent. "Self-defense. Thank you, Mr. Brunelle, for finally realizing what you are constitutionally required to prove before attempting to deprive my client of his dearly held liberty. RCW 9A.16.050—titled appropriately enough, 'Homicide, When Justifiable'—sets out, with remarkable clarity and specificity, the additional elements which the State must prove in a self-defense case, and prove beyond a reasonable doubt."

"And this is a self-defense case," Judge Daniels half-asked, half-acknowledged. She'd read the factual summary in the probable cause declaration.

"It may be," Brunelle put in. "Or maybe it's not."

Welles turned to Brunelle with a genuinely surprised expression. "You know my client claimed self-defense when he was interrogated by the police."

"And you know," Brunelle returned, "that I don't have to introduce that at trial. I'm not likely to introduce a defendant's self-serving statement that he acted in self-defense. And under the evidence rules, I can block you from eliciting it from the cops yourself. That means it's not a self-defense case until and unless your guy takes the stand and says it is. And we're a long way from the trial."

Welles's expression traveled from surprise, to appraisal, to a barely perceptible flash of anger, before moving quickly to frustration and finally admiration. But he wasn't about to concede.

"You see, Your Honor?" he spun Brunelle's response. "The State admits that it knew self-defense is an issue in this case, and still it chose to ignore the plain requirements of the Revised Code of Washington. The Court should find that the information filed this morning by Mr. Brunelle is legally insufficient and release Mr. Nguyen immediately. He can always be summoned back to court when and if Mr. Brunelle figures out how to file the charges properly."

Daniels nodded at Welles. "Thank you, counsel. I appreciate your advocacy. And I am impressed with your knowledge of both the facts and the law relevant to this case even at this earliest of junctures. Your motion is denied."

Welles didn't miss a beat. He nodded and smiled, almost as if the judge had granted his motion. "Thank you, Your Honor. Mr. Nguyen pleads not guilty. We would like to be heard regarding bail."

Brunelle breathed a small sigh of relief—one he hoped wasn't perceptible to the others in the courtroom, especially Welles. Then he readied himself for the judge to turn to him and ask, "What is the State asking regarding bail and conditions of release?"

"Thank you, Your Honor," he replied, to buy a moment to gather his thoughts again. "The State recommends the Court set bail in the amount of one million dollars. We would also ask for no contact with the family of the victim, uh..." He looked down at the information to remind himself of the victim's name. "Peter Ostrander." He pronounced it *OH-strander*, but then corrected himself. "Er, Ostrander," he tried, saying it *AH-strander*. "Yeah, probably 'Ah-strander.' Peter 'Ah-strander.'"

"Yeah, probably 'Ah-strander,'" Welles agreed under his breath.

Brunelle shook his head and frowned. Murder cases always seemed to take on the name of the defendant. This one was State v. Nguyen, or the Nguyen case. His last one had been the Rappaport case. Before that was the Hernandez case, and the Brown case, the Atkins case. The victim's name always took a back seat to the defendant's, at least for the lawyers and court staff, because all the pleadings and calendars and subpoenas always had the defendant's name on them, not the victim's. Brunelle tried not to let himself fall into that pattern, but sometimes he failed. And sometimes he failed in open court, in front of a court reporter and everyone.

The judge turned to Welles. "Any argument regarding bail, Mr. Welles?"

"Yes, Your Honor," Welles responded crisply. "We would ask the Court to release Mr. Nguyen on his own recognizance. As the Court is well aware, I'm sure, the court rules establish a presumption of a personal recognizance release. Criminal Rule 3.2 specifically states that the only bases to hold an accused are a risk of flight or danger to the community. In this case, Mr. Nguyen was born and raised in Seattle. His entire family lives in the area. He is not a flight risk. As for being a danger to the community, well," Welles scoffed lightly, "regardless of what the State wants to admit to today, this is a self-defense case. That means it was a very specific set of facts, unlikely to be repeated, and during which Mr. Nguyen was acting fully within his rights. He is no more a threat to the community than anyone else who would seek to use lawful force to defend themselves or others against the risk of substantial bodily harm or even death. There is no basis to hold my client, and without any such basis the Court should, nay, must, release Mr. Nguyen during the pendency of this case."

Brunelle smiled inside. Never tell a judge what she 'must' do. They'll show you they don't have to either, just to prove their superiority over the lawyers. Prior public defender or not, Daniels was a judge now. And it was, until her rotation ended at least, her courtroom.

"Bail will be set at five hundred thousand dollars," she ruled. The million Brunelle had asked for, but with a 50% self-defense discount. Exactly what Brunelle had expected. "In addition," the judge continued, "the defendant will have no criminal law violations and will have no contact with the family of Peter Ostrander."

Then, in case Welles didn't know it was over, Judge Daniels looked over to that young prosecutor who was handling the morning's docket. "Next case," she instructed.

The arraignment was over, and Welles was denied further audience. Plus, he needed to go back into the holding cells with his client to discuss what had just happened and what to do next. That freed Brunelle to leave the courtroom as well and head back to his office to tackle the rest of his day. But as he passed through the crowded gallery, the next part of his day stood up and presented itself.

"Excuse me, sir," a late middle-aged man with white hair and mustache stepped out from the benches. "You're the prosecutor, right? I'm Jim Ostrander."

He pronounced it with an 'Oh' at the front after all. *Damn*, Brunelle thought.

"I'm Pete's dad," the man confirmed his relation to the case, then pointed to the woman with gray-streaked red hair who stood up behind him. "This is Pete's mom, Sue. Do you have a minute to talk with us about what's happening?"

Did he have a minute to talk with the parents of the murder victim, whose name he had just mispronounced in open court? Brunelle reached out to shake Mr. OH-strander's hand.

"Of course," he said. "It would be an honor."

CHAPTER 7

'Honor' was probably too strong of a word, but Brunelle felt a need to make up for mispronouncing the name of the Ostranders' dead child. He managed to make small talk about the lack of parking near the courthouse as they took the elevator to the Prosecutor's Office. The receptionist waved them through the security door and Brunelle led them through the maze of hallways and cubicles to his office. As he made the last turn, his legal secretary, Nicole Richards, saw him from her desk and opened her mouth as if to say something, but then closed it again as the Ostranders came into view behind him. It was one thing to jump on him as soon as he got back from court—that was standard—it was another to interrupt a meeting with the victim family. Especially parents.

"Here we are," Brunelle announced as they reached his office. It didn't quite have the view boasted by the corner office of his boss, the elected District Attorney, but it wasn't terrible either. Seattle was a pretty town, especially when seen from a couple dozen stories up. He gestured to the guest chairs. "Please, have a seat."

Jim and Sue Ostrander sat down opposite Brunelle as he lowered himself into his own chair. They seemed uncomfortable, like everything they touched hurt just a little bit. He'd seen it before. The immensity of the tragedy of losing a child created an almost palpable physical sensitivity.

Nothing felt right. Because nothing was right.

"First, let me apologize for mispronouncing your last name," Brunelle led off. He could at least try to make one small thing right. "Everything I get at the beginning is written, so I don't always know how to pronounce names."

Jim waived off the apology. "Don't worry about it. It happens all the time. At least you pronounced Peter right," he tried for a joke. But his expression didn't carry it well. And Sue's even less so. She fought back tears.

"Peter," she echoed, a quiet wail. "Pete. My little Petey. Oh my God, what happened, Mr. Brunelle? Do you know what happened?"

Brunelle sighed. He didn't know. Not everything. Not yet. And what he did know wasn't likely to make them feel any better. '*It looks like your son lost a shoot-out over a girl*' probably wouldn't go over very well.

"We're still gathering all the information," Brunelle answered instead. "I'd like to have more information before I start guessing as to exactly what happened, or why. But I can tell you this: we arrested the person who killed your son, and we will do everything in our power to make sure he's held accountable."

That's what they wanted to hear.

Jim nodded and looked to Sue, who offered a weak nod in reply.

"What was all that about self-defense?" Sue asked after a moment.

"Yeah," Jim agreed. "Are they claiming self-defense?"

"Probably," Brunelle hedged his answer. "But we'll have to wait and see if they follow through with that. There are really only two ways to defend a murder charge: say you didn't do it, or say you had to do it. There are reasons to believe he might say he had to do it, but at least that means we know he did do it. We have the right person."

Again, a couple of nods from the grieving parents. Brunelle didn't expect many more questions beyond those two major inquiries, and he knew he probably couldn't answer them anyway, so he went ahead and started to wrap it up. The value in the meeting was having it at all—being available for the grieving parents. But he couldn't share information with them, and he couldn't bring their son back. And he had work to do.

"So, let me tell you what happens next," he started.

They seemed out of their element in the courthouse. Not every grieving family member was. A lot of them, in fact, had come through the system themselves, more than once. But Jim and Sue Ostrander seemed like the kind of suburban parents who only came to the courthouse to get copies of the kids' birth certificates so they could get the passports for that trip to Europe. They probably didn't even know about their son's own handful of arrests for drug possession. At least they didn't seem to, and right then really wasn't the time to bring it up, Brunelle knew. Instead, he guessed they could benefit from a crash course in criminal procedure.

He explained that it would be a while until the trial, but that there would be several court dates before then. Most were just pretrial conferences for the lawyers to talk and no need for them to attend. There might be motions to suppress evidence, but Brunelle would be ready for them. And finally, after all of the preliminary work was done, the trial would commence. Unless, the defendant pled guilty. But Brunelle knew Jeremy Nguyen wasn't going to plead guilty. Not when he started with 'Self-defense!' And not with Welles as his attorney.

"I can't promise what a jury will do," Brunelle concluded, "but I can promise that I will do everything in my power to hold Pete's killer responsible."

Jim and Sue looked at each other and squeezed each other's hand. "Thank you, Mr. Brunelle," Sue said. "That's all we can ask for."

"Yes, thank you for taking the time to meet with us," Jim said as they all stood up and started shaking hands. "It was very nice to meet you."

Brunelle returned the sentiment. "It was nice to meet you too." He handed each of them a business card from his top drawer. "If you have any further questions, please don't hesitate to contact me directly."

A few more 'thank you's and Brunelle guided them out of his office and back to the lobby. That was likely the last time he'd talk to them until the eve of trial, unless they really did have more questions. And they were the type of questions he couldn't shove off onto his legal secretary.

"I hate those meetings," Brunelle said after he turned the corner again and stopped at the desk of that legal secretary. "I can't promise a conviction—that's unethical. And I can't bring their kid back. So, it's just about the tragedy and how helpless we all are to do anything about it."

"Sure." Nicole nodded, a bit coldly. "But I can tell you this: it won't be the worst meeting you have this morning."

Brunelle frowned. "What are you talking about? You're not quitting, are you?"

Nicole raised her eyebrows and chuckled. "Oh, no, Dave, it's not my job we're talking about."

"Whose job are we talking about?" Brunelle asked, not sure he wanted to know the answer.

But Nicole demurred. "Nope. I've said too much already. Matt wants to see you in his office as soon as possible."

"Matt?" Matt Duncan. That elected D.A. boss with the corner office. "Matt wants to see me?"

"Yes, sir," Nicole confirmed. "I told him you were meeting with a victim family, so he's waiting. He told me to tell you to go to his office as soon as you finished."

Brunelle's shoulders fell. "And I'm finished."

"May be," Nicole joked. "Go and find out."

Brunelle had no idea why Duncan would want to see him just then. He hadn't briefed him on the Nguyen case—the Ostrander case—but it wasn't likely to be a big media case, so there was no need. But what else could it be?

He buttoned up his suit coat and straightened his tie, then headed for Duncan's office at the end of the hall. Duncan had his own administrative assistant, who smiled encouragingly at Brunelle when he arrived at her desk.

"Go on in," she said with a nod toward the door of Duncan's office. "They're waiting for you."

They? Brunelle thought to himself as he circled the desk and headed for Duncan's office.

As he stepped inside, Duncan shot to his feet behind his desk. "Dave," he said even as he pointed to the woman seated across from him who also stood up at his entrance. "This is Carmen Saint James from County Human Resources."

"Good morning, Mr. Brunelle," Saint James said with an unconvincing smile. "I'm here because a complaint has been filed against you."

Brunelle stopped in his tracks. "A complaint?" he parroted. "For what?"

Saint James's smile evaporated. "Sexual harassment."

CHAPTER 8

Brunelle stood stock still in the door frame, shell shocked by the accusation. But it only took a moment for his trial attorney's mind to come back to life and begin processing the possibilities.

It was County H.R., which meant it was a county employee who had complained. A non-county employee could sue, but not file an internal complaint. So, that limited the possible suspects.

Kat? No, Chen said she'd left for California.

Robyn? No, she left the Public Defender's Office for private practice.

Nicole? Gosh, he hoped not. He always thought they were friends. If he offended her, she'd just tell him. Wouldn't she?

Gwen? Ha. She'd be more likely to get a complaint filed against her than Brunelle.

Michelle? Maybe. She had a history of these sort of complaints, but it had been a while since they'd worked together.

Brunelle paused his mental rundown of possible suspects. *Wow, there are a lot of names on that list,* he realized. *Maybe there's something to this.*

He shook his head and opened his palms. "What?"

"Sexual harassment," Saint James repeated.

"I heard that," Brunelle replied. "But what is this all about?"

He wanted to hear the allegation. So he could refute it. He knew—like every criminal lawyer and every cop knew—talking never helped. If you have something to say, you can say it later. To the jury. After you've huddled with your lawyer. But he also knew—like every criminal lawyer and every cop also knew—almost everybody talked anyway. Even after they got their Miranda warnings. It was human nature. People want to tell their side of the story. They want to talk their way out of things. On the other hand, in real life—not criminal cases—refusing to deny something was usually treated the same as admitting it. Brunelle knew to react carefully when he heard the allegation. The only question he really had was whether he'd be able to deny it.

"Sit down, Dave." Duncan gestured to the seat next to Saint James.

Brunelle took it, but pulled the chair several inches away from her and turned it so he was more facing her than sitting next to her.

"Can you just tell me what this is all about?" Brunelle asked again. "What's the allegation? Who filed the complaint?"

"Normally," Saint James replied, "we don't reveal the identity of the complainant. However, in this case, the complainant has authorized the disclosure of her identity."

"Great," Brunelle said impatiently. "Who is it? And what did I do? I'm really at a loss."

"The complainant," Saint James finally answered, but slowly, "is Dr. Marianne Delacourt of the County Medical Examiner's Office."

"What?!" Brunelle practically shouted. But he laughed as well. "I've had like two interactions with her. Ever. I only just met her."

"Okay, calm down, Dave," Duncan raised a calming hand at him. "What specifically is the allegation?" he asked Saint James.

"Mr. Brunelle demeaned and degraded the doctor," Saint James answered, "by referring to her as a 'girl.'"

Brunelle took a moment to process the information. He probably should have taken another moment to consider his response. "Are you fucking kidding me? I didn't call her a girl."

"I suppose that's partially correct," Saint James replied. "You called her a 'pretty girl.' But that doesn't really help matters, Mr. Brunelle."

Brunelle sighed and ran a hand over his head, only slightly mussing his shortly cropped hair. "Look. I didn't mean to offend anyone. I thought she was someone else and I was making a joke. I guess it wasn't very funny. Obviously. But it wasn't malicious."

"Who did you think she was?" Saint James asked.

Another sigh. "An ex-girlfriend."

"Kat?" Duncan realized, eyes wide. "Oh, Dave."

Brunelle cocked his head at his boss. "You knew about me and Kat?"

"Everyone knew about that," Duncan answered. "You're not exactly a discrete person."

"I can be private," Brunelle protested.

Duncan shook his head. "Not the same thing."

Brunelle just frowned. "Look. I thought she was an ex-girlfriend. I was awkward, so I made a bad joke. I meant no disrespect to Dr. Delacourt. And I certainly wasn't sexually harassing her."

"We'll be the judge of what constitutes sexual harassment, Mr. Brunelle," Saint James replied. "In any event, this meeting was simply to inform you of the complaint, Mr. Brunelle. We will be conducting a formal investigation and we expect you to cooperate with that. In the meantime, you are to have no contact with the complainant, Dr. Delacourt."

Brunelle's brows knitted together. "She's the M.E. on my latest case. She did the autopsy. I'm going to need to talk to her at some point, even if it's just asking her questions on the stand."

Then he realized one possible solution. He turned to Duncan. "Matt, no. Don't take me off this case. I was at the scene, the interrogation. I did the arraignment just this morning. Shit, Matt, I just met with the parents. I promised them I'd do everything I could to hold their son's killer responsible. You can't take the case away from me. Not now. This is all just a big misunderstanding."

But Saint James answered instead of Duncan. "Dr. Delacourt anticipated this issue," she said. "She instructed another pathologist at the

Medical Examiner's Office to review her autopsy and be ready to testify in her place. She doesn't want your personal actions to jeopardize the criminal prosecution."

"My personal actions?" Brunelle leaned forward. "Now, you listen here—"

But Duncan interjected. "That's enough for now, Dave." He turned to his other guest. "Thank you for coming, Ms. Saint James. I'll speak with Mr. Brunelle and we'll get this straightened out. I promise Dave and our entire office will cooperate fully with Human Resources to bring this to an expeditious conclusion."

Brunelle couldn't quite restrain a sneer, but he managed to bite his tongue.

Saint James thanked Duncan, nodded curtly to Brunelle, and departed, leaving Brunelle fuming across the desk from Duncan.

"Are you fucking kidding me?" Brunelle let out once the office door closed behind the H.R. rep. "This is total bullshit. It was a fucking joke."

"Yeah, well, this investigation is no joke," Duncan replied. "I meant it when I said we would cooperate fully."

"Of course," Brunelle waved a hand dismissively at Duncan. Then he regained himself slightly. Never smart to be rude to the boss. "I mean, right. I know. Of course." He sighed. "Thanks for letting me keep the Ostrander case. This would be a stupid reason to have a case taken away."

"It would be a stupid comment to make to force me to take it away," Duncan reframed the issue. "You can thank Dr. Delacourt for passing the case to another M.E."

"You can thank her," Brunelle returned. "I'm not allowed to talk to her."

He shook his head. "Sorry about all this, Matt. But I promise, I won't let it affect how I handle the case. The defendant has already hired William Harrison Welles. I'm going to have plenty to deal with from him, so I should manage to avoid saying anything else stupid."

But Duncan just laughed. "Too late. You just did. And you will again.

Especially with Welles pushing your buttons."

Brunelle raised his chin. "I can handle Welles."

"I know you can," Duncan answered. "But I need you squeaky clean on this one. That's why I already picked your second-chair."

"My second-chair?" Brunelle complained. "Let me take a look at the case again, Matt. I'm not sure I need a second prosecutor to help me with it."

"Maybe not," Duncan conceded, "but I need one to help me help you stay out of trouble."

Brunelle shrugged. "What about Gwen Carlisle? We get along."

"No, she'll get you into more trouble." Duncan shook his head. "No, I'm pairing you up with someone who will be a good influence on you."

"Who?" Brunelle braced himself.

"Gregory Meckle," Duncan answered. "Do you know him?"

Brunelle pinched the bridge of his nose. "Meckle? Yeah. I've met him."

Gregory Meckle was one of the most earnestly, genuinely, aggravatingly nice people Brunelle had ever had the displeasure of having to tolerate. He was polite to a fault, calling everyone by Mr. or Mrs., even friends he'd known since law school. And he was at that point in his career arc when it was time for him to dip a toe in the homicide pool. Brunelle just wished he didn't have to be the lifeguard. At a real pool, Brunelle probably would have let him drown, letting his cries of '*Excuse me, Mr. Lifeguard, sir, but could you help me?*' sink beneath the surface.

"Not only will he be a good influence on you," Duncan beamed, "but he will have no hesitation reporting back to me anything and everything you shouldn't be doing."

Brunelle grimaced. "Is there any way I can get out of trying the case with Meckle?" He figured he'd ask.

"Give up the case," Duncan answered. "I can inflict Meckle on Fletcher instead."

As appealing as that sounded—Brunelle didn't like Fletcher much either—he wasn't one to give up a case. Especially after he'd made a promise to the parents.

"I'm looking forward to working with Gregory," Brunelle announced as he stood up. Then he asked, "Does he go by Greg?"

Duncan shook his head. "Nope. Gregory."

Brunelle sighed yet again. "Figures."

CHAPTER 9

Meckle's office was on the same floor as Gwen Carlisle's. She would have made a great second-chair. She had made a great second-chair. A white guy took a bullet between the eyes under an overpass in Chinatown. That was just crying out for the kind of insensitive jokes and double entendres Carlisle was expert at. Which, Brunelle knew, was exactly why he had to walk past her office and force himself to march down the hallway to Meckle's.

But that didn't mean he couldn't stop real quick and say hi.

He knocked on her door frame. "Hey, Gwen?"

Carlisle looked every bit the part of rock-solid trial partner. Dark suit, cream blouse, brown hair cut stylishly just above the shoulder. She looked up from whatever she was hard at work on. "Yes?"

"You wanna do a murder trial with me?"

Carlisle slapped her desktop. "Fuck, yeah!"

"Yeah, me too," Brunelle answered. "But Matt says I have to do it with Meckle."

"Meckle?" Carlisle practically gagged on the name. "He's soooo boring. And obsequious." She closed her eyes and pretended to fall asleep. "Hello, Mr. Sheep, sir. May I count you and your Mr. and Mrs. Friends? Mr. One... Mrs. Two... Professor Three... Dominatrix Four..."

"Whoa," Brunelle laughed. "What's up with that fourth sheep? I didn't think Dominatrix was a title."

"I think it's usually 'Madame'," Carlisle agreed. "But you wouldn't have gotten the joke if I'd just said 'Madame.'"

"You think?" Brunelle challenged.

Carlisle grinned. "That's my story…"

Brunelle sighed at her. "And you're sure you're not even a little bit straight?"

Carlisle laughed. "Not even a little bit. But watch yourself, Mr. Brunelle, you keep asking questions like that and you could end up with an H.R. complaint."

Brunelle's own grin melted away. "Actually, I already have one."

"What?" Carlisle gasped. "Oh my God, what happened? Spill!"

So Brunelle told her the story from the beginning, although light on the details of his relationship with Kat.

When he finished, Carlisle shook her head. "That's not sexual harassment," she said.

"I know," Brunelle agreed.

"It's not even funny," Carlisle added.

"Uh…"

"So, that's why you got paired with Captain Somnambulance? Awesome. I don't know what they're going to do to you, but that should be punishment enough. Enjoy!"

Brunelle sighed. "Maybe next case?" he tried.

"Maybe," Carlisle agreed, "if you can keep that sexist attitude of yours in your pants."

Brunelle cocked his head at her. "That doesn't even make sense."

"I know," Gwen admitted. Then she pointed toward the door. "Now, scat. I have work to do, and you have a terrible, boring, obsequious second-chair to recruit."

Brunelle's shoulders dropped. "Thanks, Gwen. It's always nice to see you."

"Fuck you too, Dave," Carlisle answered, and she waved him out of her office.

Brunelle walked the hallway slowly, in no hurry to exchange the gregarious and inappropriate Gwen Carlisle for a man who probably called his own parents by their last names. But Duncan was the boss, and an order was an order.

"Hey, Greg," Brunelle greeted him as he knocked on his open door frame. Then he remembered to add, "—Ory. Greg*ory*. Hey, Gregory. How's it going?"

Meckle looked up from his computer screen. He was young and thin, almost slight, with a baby face and curling brown hair that needed a trim. He had no glasses or facial hair. Brunelle wondered if he still went a few days between shaving.

"Oh, hello, Mr. Brunelle," Meckle chirped from behind his desk. "How are you today? How can I help you?"

Brunelle tried to force his grimace into a smile. "Call me Dave. And I'm here to see if you'd like to help me out on a case."

Meckle turned fully away from his computer and stood up. "Really, Mr. Brunelle? One of your cases? A murder case?"

Brunelle nodded. "Yep." He almost said, 'Yeppers.' The word 'golly' also popped into his head. Maybe it was contagious. He decided not to touch anything.

"Uh, yeah," Brunelle answered. "A murder case. Matt suggested you. He thinks you're ready to work on a homicide case."

"Mr. Duncan said that?" Meckle confirmed. "Golly. That's just great. Wow, thank you, Mr. Brunelle. I promise, I won't let you down."

"Right," Brunelle replied. "Like I said, call me Dave. And I know you won't."

"So, what's the case about, Mr. Brunelle?" Meckle asked with wide eyes.

Brunelle took a deep breath. "You know what? Why don't you just contact Nicole Richards, one of the legal assistants in Homicides? Tell her you're my second-chair on this case. She'll give you copies of all the police reports. Read those, and then we'll talk."

Meckle nodded enthusiastically. "Yes, sir, Mr. Brunelle. Is there anything else I should know?"

Brunelle considered. "Yeah, there is."

"What?"

"We just did the arraignment," Brunelle explained. "Get a copy of the transcript and read it."

Meckle's smile faded slightly. He cocked his head. "Couldn't you just tell me, Mr. Brunelle?"

Brunelle finally offered a genuine grin himself before turning to leave. "Yeah, Greg. I could."

CHAPTER 10

Asking around Chinatown.

That sounded good to Brunelle, and not just because of the cadence and internal near-rhyme. Self-defense and love triangles didn't fit well together. Self-defense was more of an 'in the moment' type of thing. Confronting your lover's other lover? That's more of a premeditated thing. You can't confront someone and then cause a situation that requires you to act in self-defense. Really, you can't. Not in Washington anyway. It was called the first aggressor rule and it was a standard jury instruction in all self-defense cases. Brunelle knew that, and so did Welles. So, Brunelle needed evidence of the love triangle.

The problem was, the three main witnesses to that love triangle weren't talking. Jeremy Nguyen, because Welles wouldn't let him. Peter Ostrander, because he was dead. And Joan Inha, because Brunelle had no idea who or where she was.

Well, he had one idea: Chinatown.

Or rather, the International District, which was only a few blocks from the courthouse. Brunelle needed to eat lunch anyway and there were literally dozens of restaurants there. He figured he'd start with miso soup and questions at one end of the neighborhood, make his way thru some fried rice and questions in the middle, and end with some kung pao chicken and questions at the far end. Then maybe take an Uber back. It wasn't that close to the courthouse.

But no one at the noodle house knew a Joan Inha. She also wasn't known to any of the wait staff at the teriyaki joint. He even tried at the Starbucks on the way to his final destination, The Jade House, but no luck with the barista either. Unfortunately, all that snacking and asking meant he didn't get to The Jade House before the lunch rush. There was already a line out the door.

Brunelle really didn't want to wait in line. But he did really want to eat. And eat at The Jade House. They had the best kung pao chicken in Seattle. And if he left to try somewhere else, they'd probably have a line too, and it would take even longer. He sighed, but then stepped up on the curb and took his place in line. He didn't have afternoon court, so it would be okay if he got back to his desk late. And he was still kind of working— looking for the increasingly elusive Joan Inha.

He peered in the windows, imagining that one of the waitresses might even be Joan. Maybe Peter Ostrander had met her when he'd gone there for dinner one night. Maybe Jeremy Nguyen was her jealous ex-boyfriend. They were only a few blocks from the overpass. It wasn't impossible.

He was just realizing, seeing his own ghostly reflection bobbing its head in the window glass, that he probably looked a little strange, when the woman behind him in line confirmed it.

"So," she asked, "what's a super-white narc like you doing at a great Asian restaurant like this?"

Brunelle ripped his gaze from the restaurant window and regarded the woman behind him, standing several inches shorter, and several years younger, than him. She was white too, with short blonde hair, hanging in thick loose curls, and an elaborate tattoo that circled part of her neck, before disappearing beneath her shirt and reappearing, he presumed, at her wrist. Her eyes were hidden behind sunglasses, but her full lips were still smiling at her own joke

"Pardon me?" he stammered.

"Wow, even whiter," the woman said. "And narckier."

Brunelle took a moment, then looked down at what he was wearing. A suit. No one wore suits any more. Not in Seattle, anyway. When he'd started out as a young lawyer, he used to joke that only bankers and lawyers still wore suits. But the bankers had long ago moved to khakis, as had the lawyers whose practices didn't involve going to court. That left trial lawyers. And narcs, apparently.

"The suit, right?" he asked.

"Yeah." She laughed. "And the 'pardon me.' Plus, peering in the window like you were looking for a perp or something."

"Perp?" Brunelle parroted. "Now you sound like the narc."

The woman grinned at that. "I'm no narc. I promise. But seriously, are you a cop or something?"

"No," Brunelle felt compelled to defend. "I'm a lawyer. A prosecutor, actually." He gestured at his attire. "I go to court a lot."

The woman nodded approvingly. "Okay, that makes sense. You're a lawyer who works for the narcs, and so you gotta look the part."

Brunelle wasn't immediately sure how to respond. In part, because she wasn't completely wrong. So instead of responding, he stuck out his hand. "I'm Dave. Nice to meet you."

"Abbie," the woman said as she shook his hand. "Even if you are a narc."

"A lawyer who works for the narcs," Brunelle corrected. "I take it, you don't like cops?"

Abbie shrugged. "No, I like everybody. Just trying to figure you out. You kinda stick out, you know? And the peeping Tom routine doesn't help."

Brunelle shrugged. He supposed she was right.

The line was shuffling forward and they repositioned themselves closer to the door as another party was seated.

"So, are you looking for a criminal?" Abbie repeated.

"No." Brunelle shook his head. "A witness. You don't happen to know anyone named Joan who lives or works around here, do you?"

"Joan?" Abbie repeated the name. "I don't think so."

"Do you live around here?" Brunelle asked. It really was for informational purposes—to see if she had the background knowledge to be a credible source.

But Abbie lowered her eyebrows behind her sunglasses. "I don't tell strange men I've just met where I live."

Brunelle's own eyebrows rose. "Oh, right. Sorry. I just meant, you know, if you lived around here, you might know her, or not, I guess. I don't know. Sorry."

Abbie shrugged it off with another bright grin. "No worries. I work around here," she explained, gesturing generally in the direction of where Peter Ostrander's body had been found. "But I don't know any Joan. Sorry."

Another party went inside and Brunelle was at the head of the line.

"Is she a witness to something important?" Abbie asked.

Brunelle nodded. "A murder. I think."

Abbie cocked her head. "You think it was a murder? Wouldn't you kind of know?"

"I think she's a witness to the murder," Brunelle clarified. "But actually," he continued, "whether a homicide is a murder or not is a legal question. It's only a murder if it's illegal. So, if it's justified, like self-defense, then it's not murder. So, in that way, I guess I do think it was murder, not just homicide."

Abbie nodded for several seconds. "Yeah, pretty narcky. Do you ever do anything for fun?"

Before Brunelle could answer, the hostess stepped outside. "Table ready!" she barked.

Brunelle looked between the hostess and Abbie. "Uh, table for two?" he ventured.

But no such luck. "No," the hostess answered. "One chair. At table with other people. You want it or no?"

Brunelle looked back at the compelling young woman he'd just met.

But she waved him inside. "Go on, Dave. This place is always packed. You better take the spot. I'm gonna get mine to go anyway. But maybe we'll run into each other again."

Brunelle nodded. He sure hoped so.

CHAPTER 11

It was a few days later when it finally happened. Brunelle knew it was coming. Ever since the arraignment.

"Legal messenger just dropped this off," Nicole announced as Brunelle turned the corner toward his office that morning. She held a pleading in her hand. "It's on the Nguyen case."

"The Ostrander case," Brunelle corrected, only half-joking. He stepped over and took the papers from Nicole. "Motion to Dismiss," he read aloud.

"The usual garbage, right?" Nicole asked.

Brunelle scanned the first page of the document to confirm his expectations. "No, unique garbage. Welles's specialty."

"So, you don't have a stock response brief?" Nicole inquired.

Nope," Brunelle admitted. "But I have something better."

"What's that?"

"A second-chair." He turned back toward the stairwell, the brief clutched in his hand. "If anyone's looking for me, I'll be in Meckle's office."

On his way to the stairwell, Brunelle read the brief more thoroughly. It was based on the *State v. Knapstad*, a case every criminal practitioner in Washington knew. It stood for the proposition that a case had to be dismissed if you assumed everything the prosecution alleged was true but it still didn't amount to a crime. In the original case, Mr. Knapstad was charged with growing marijuana—at *his brother's* house. Prior to trial, he moved to dismiss the case, arguing the prosecution couldn't prove he knew anything about what his brother was doing there. The prosecution argued that they could at least try, and if they failed, then the jury would just acquit him. The trial judge didn't think that was a particularly good use of resources, or a particularly fair way to treat a defendant, and dismissed the case prior to trial. Ever since then, a '*Knapstad* motion' was made any time a defense attorney believed the State didn't have the evidence to prove the charges.

But it wasn't usually applicable in a murder case. In a murder case, there was a dead body (usually), and a defendant who'd been connected (somehow) to the body being dead. Assuming the truth of the State's allegation usually meant a conviction, so Knapstad just never applied.

But then came William Harrison Welles. And Jeremy Nguyen.

The elements of murder in the first degree were usually the premeditated killing of another person. That was it. Unless the defendant asserted self-defense, in which case the State also had to prove, beyond a reasonable doubt, that it wasn't self-defense. Welles's motion argued that there was insufficient evidence in the police reports to disprove self-defense, and therefore, the Court should dismiss the charges outright. It was the logical extension of his argument at arraignment.

When Brunelle arrived at Meckle's office, his co-counsel was staring at his computer screen, typing something to someone about something else.

"Greg," Brunelle interrupted his thoughts.

Meckle jerked his head up. "Oh. Mr. Brunelle. Hello." He stood up, as if a judge had just entered the courtroom. "What can I do for you?"

"Did you get the transcript of the arraignment?" Brunelle asked.

"Yes, sir," Meckle replied.

"Did you read it?"

"Yes, sir."

"Did you understand it?"

"Yes, Mr. Brunelle."

Brunelle rolled his eyes. "Dave," he tried one more time. Then, he clarified his question. "Did you understand why Welles thought he was right?"

"Uh, I think I understood his argument," Meckle hedged.

"Do you understand why he was wrong?"

"Yes, Mr. Brunelle. I think so."

"Good," Brunelle said. He threw the motion to dismiss on Meckle's desk. "Write the response brief to this. The judge needs to understand it too."

CHAPTER 12

There were several reasons why Brunelle had Meckle write the response brief. One reason was simply that he didn't want to do it. Brunelle liked courtroom work, not desk work. But Meckle seemed like the kind of lawyer who might enjoy reading case after case and editing written arguments over and over. Another reason was that Meckle needed to understand the biggest weakness in their case, so he could help Brunelle overcome it. If Brunelle was going to be in a foxhole with Meckle, he wanted Meckle armed. And a third reason was that Brunelle had other things to do on the case, things that required him to leave his office and computer behind.

"Is Detective Chen in?" he asked the officer of the day, stationed behind the bulletproof glass of the reception desk of Seattle Police Department headquarters.

"And your name, sir?" the officer asked back, without answering Brunelle's question.

"Dave Brunelle. I'm with the King County Prosecutor's Office. He knows me."

"Yes, sir," the officer replied, with more politeness than his original response. Brunelle didn't really care. The officer undoubtedly spent his day dealing with angry and/or mentally ill citizens who demanded to see the Chief, or the Assistant Chief, or the Bat Signal, depending on what drugs they were on at that moment. Then again, Brunelle was in his narc outfit, so the officer should have known he was serious.

The officer set down the phone he'd picked up to confirm Chen's availability and nodded to Brunelle. "He'll be right out, Mr. Brunelle."

Brunelle thanked the officer and stepped away from the reception desk. *See*, he thought, *that was the correct use of 'Mr. Brunelle.'*

It only took a few minutes for Chen to appear in the lobby, and one more for them to walk back to his office.

"So, what's up?" the detective asked as they both sat down in his office. It was cramped and cluttered, already too small for the large man who occupied it, and stuffed with papers and binders and boxes. "This about the Nguyen case?"

Brunelle decided not to correct him with another 'the Ostrander case,' although he was tempted. "Yeah," he agreed. "I was wondering if you'd found our elusive Ms. Inha yet?"

Chen frowned and shook his head. "No, sorry, Dave. Not yet."

"Have you tried?" Brunelle asked. Then, realizing that sounded harsher than he intended, "I mean, have you had time?"

Chen chuckled and gestured around his office. "I never have time, Dave, but I make time somehow. I have to."

"So, where are we then?" Brunelle followed up. "This is a really important part of the case. I need to explain to the jury why Nguyen would have shot Ostrander. I mean, I would need to explain that anyway, but it's especially important here where Nguyen is going to claim self-defense. The problem I have is that he gets to testify after I rest my case, so if I don't have a motive, he's got a blank check to say whatever he wants. I really need to find this woman."

"Understood," Chen replied, but with a casualness that made Brunelle question it. "I did all the usual stuff. All the databases. But there's no one with that name. No criminal records, no driver's license records, not even any rental applications."

"Undocumented?" Brunelle proposed.

"Maybe." Chen shrugged. "Or maybe Joan isn't her real name. A lot of Asian families give their children traditional first names. Mine was Yong until I did a formal name change in high school. Everyone called me by my English name anyway. But if she's not using her real name on anything, then I can't really find her with only a name, can I?"

Brunelle frowned, but had to concede the point. "What about asking around the International District?" Brunelle hadn't had any luck, but then again, he wasn't a detective. Badges and guns had a way of being more persuasive than suits and ties.

But Chen shook his head. "That's needle in the haystack stuff, Dave. And do you know what the problem with needles in haystacks is? It's not that you won't find the needle. You'll find it if you take your time. The problem is how much damn time you have to take." He gestured again at his office full of papers, files, and boxes. "I don't have that kind of time. Not right now. The brass is trying to clear out some of our cold cases. Every detective got ten cases we have to either solve or close, and I don't want to close any without being solved."

"The Ostrander case might go unsolved," Brunelle challenged, "if we don't find Joan Inha."

But Chen just cocked his head and chuckled. "The Ostrander case was solved that night when we arrested Nguyen. He did it. Case solved. Now, whether you can get a conviction, well, that's a different issue."

"Isn't that the most important issue?" Brunelle asked.

Chen shrugged again. "Probably. But it's your issue. Not mine. Even if he's acquitted, we still solved the case. It's not like there's somebody else out there who might have done it."

"What about Joan Inha?" Brunelle said. "She's still out there."

"Yeah, but she didn't do it," Chen answered. "Nguyen may not have said much, but he did say 'self-defense.' Self-defense means he did it. Case solved."

Brunelle just shook his head. "I really need her, Larry. Solved isn't enough. He needs to be held responsible. You can't just give up because she wasn't in a few government databases. I feel like you're not being much of a partner on this."

Chen lowered his brow. "Okay. Well, that sounds like we're married or something. Look, I'm doing what I can. I've got a few more angles. I'll check with the other detectives. Maybe vice has a line on someone with that name. But I think you better get ready to try the case without her. Or else, find a partner who will drop everything and do whatever you say."

Brunelle nodded. "Good idea."

CHAPTER 13

"Hey, Greg!" Brunelle shouted from Meckle's doorway. Then, again he added, "-Ory. Gregory."

Meckle looked up from his desk. It was covered with drafts of a brief, marked up with red ink, and printed out case law. The red pen was in his hand still. He looked tired, but he stood up anyway. "Oh, hi, Mr. Brunelle."

Brunelle sighed through his nose. "Look." He pointed at Meckle. "You and I are partners. But this is not going to work if you don't drop the Mr. Brunelle crap. Call me Dave, like everyone else in this office does."

"I'm just trying to be polite," Meckle defended.

"It's not polite," Brunelle gave back. "It's weird. You don't come across as respectful. You come across as distant and unable to interact with people in a normal way, like you're putting up a barrier or something. That isn't going to get you very far in the office, and it will get you nowhere in front of a jury."

Meckle just blinked at him.

"You want to try murder cases yourself someday, don't you?" Brunelle asked.

"Absolutely," Meckle answered.

"Then relax," Brunelle advised. "And call me 'Dave.' Or so help me, I'll give you the worst possible review to Duncan, and you'll end up doing traffic infractions for the rest of your career."

Meckle's eyes widened. "Would you really do that?"

Brunelle raised a hand to his forehead and sighed again. "No, Gregory. But I won't have to. You'll do that to yourself."

"Okay," he said. "Dave."

Brunelle smiled. "Great. Now, how's that brief coming?"

Meckle frowned at his desk. "I'm not very happy with it. It's a lot of law, but not a lot of facts."

"Don't think of them as facts," Brunelle suggested. "Think of them as a story."

"A story?" Meckle questioned.

"Right," Brunelle confirmed. "And who tells that story?"

"We do," Meckle answered.

But Brunelle shook his head. "Not quite. We retell it. But who tells us?"

Meckle considered. "The detectives?"

"Psh, I wish," Brunelle complained, recalling his meeting with Chen. "But actually, no, not really. They're retellers too. Who tells them?"

Meckle took another moment, then answered more confidently. "The witnesses."

"Exactly." Brunelle pumped a fist at him. "And who would have been the best possible witness for what happened to Peter Ostrander?"

"The defendant?" Meckle guessed.

"Yeah, well, maybe," Brunelle conceded. "But we can't call him as a witness. So, who does that leave?"

A long pause. "Peter Ostrander?"

"Yes!" Brunelle confirmed. "Peter Ostrander."

"But he's dead," Meckle pointed out.

"Yes, he is," Brunelle acknowledged. "So, who can tell the story of a dead man?"

Meckle frowned and considered. "A medium?"

Brunelle rolled his eyes. "No." He pointed at the mess on Meckle's desk. "Gather that stuff up. And grab the file. We're going on a field trip."

CHAPTER 14

Meckle had never been to the Medical Examiner's Office before. Brunelle had been there more times than he could count. He knew everyone there and they knew him. In the past, he would have just waved at the receptionist and they would have buzzed him through the secure door to go find whichever pathologist he'd come to see. But that was the past. Now, he had to check in and wait to be escorted back by the specific doctor he needed to talk to, lest he run into Dr. Marianne Delacourt and make another 'not even funny' joke which might end his career.

"Hello," Brunelle greeted the receptionist. "David Brunelle and Gregory Meckle from the Prosecutor's Office, here to see Dr. Kleinbart."

The receptionist, a young man in a tight sweater and glasses, nodded in reply. He gestured to the waiting area. "I'll let him know you're here."

Brunelle and Meckle sat down and waited for Dr. Kleinbart, but thankfully they didn't have to wait long. By the time Brunelle had picked out a months-old copy of Sport Illustrated to flip through, the door to the back offices opened and Dr. Kleinbart called out their names.

"Mr. Brunelle? Mr. Meckle? I'm Dr. Kleinbart."

Brunelle hadn't met Kleinbart before either, but he was unlikely to mistake him for a former paramour. Kleinbart was thin and short, not more than 5′ 6″, with brownish-red hair cropped almost to the skin to disguise the deeply receding hairline, a neatly trimmed beard of the same color, and thick glasses with wide black frames. His handshake was strong enough, but damp.

"Dr. Kleinbart," Brunelle said as he finished the handshake. "Thanks for taking the time to speak with us."

"Of course, of course," Kleinbart said. But then cautioned, "I don't have a lot of time before I need to get back to the examining room, but I don't think this will take very long."

Brunelle suppressed a frown. That didn't bode well for an in-depth discussion of the autopsy results.

Kleinbart's office was one of several that opened onto the hallway between the lobby and the examining rooms. They couldn't see the bodies from there, but they could smell the chemicals used to prevent anyone from having to smell anything worse.

"So, you've had a chance to review the autopsy report?" Brunelle confirmed as they all sat down.

"Dr. Delacourt's report?" Kleinbart made sure to point out. "Yes, I've reviewed her report."

"Ok," Brunelle nodded. "Good."

"Yes, I'm familiar with her report," Kleinbart went on. "I'm also familiar with the reasons why I have to be the one to testify about it."

"Ah," Brunelle replied. He supposed that wasn't a good thing.

"And I'm familiar with the limitations placed on an expert witness when testifying from the report of a different expert," he concluded. "I can report what she observed, but I cannot and will not draw any independent conclusions, especially based on hypotheticals."

"Great, great." Brunelle nodded, his tone belying his words. "Well, here's the thing. Gregory here," he gestured toward Meckle, "he hasn't tried a murder case before. So, I thought it would be beneficial to everyone if we took the time to go through the report—"

"Dr. Delacourt's report," Kleinbart interjected again.

Brunelle forced a smile. "Yes, Dr. Delacourt's report. If we took the time to go through Dr. Delacourt's report to see what information we can derive from the good doctor's findings."

"It's all in the report," Kleinbart pointed out. "And as I said, I'm familiar with the limitations placed on my testimony. I can't deviate from the report."

"Humor me," Brunelle replied. "We're not in court right now. And our job is to make sure the jury understands what Dr. Delacourt observed and the importance of those observations in the context of all of the evidence."

"Why not just introduce the report itself?" Kleinbart asked. "Then you wouldn't need me at all."

"Yeah, there are hearsay rules and Confrontation Clauses and things that frown on prosecutors just submitting expert reports to juries," Brunelle explained. "Plus, no one knows what 'anterior' means."

"It's the opposite of 'posterior,'" Kleinbart defined.

"Well done," Brunelle responded. "And that's why we need you."

Kleinbart exhaled audibly through his nose. He looked away at the clock on his wall. "I don't have that much time left. I really have to get back to my examinations. It was a busy night last night."

Gross, Brunelle thought. He was glad he didn't have to spend his days elbow-deep in cadavers. "We'll be quick," he assured the pathologist. "In fact, let's do it this way. I'll ask you a question, you answer, and Gregory," he turned to Meckle, "I want you to translate it into a part of our story."

Meckle cocked his head. "What do you mean?"

"We can't get up in front of the jury," Brunelle said, "and tell them that the subject presented a gunshot wound to the anterior torso. We tell them he got shot in the chest. Translate."

Meckle nodded, although a bit uncertainly. "Okay. Got it. I think."

Brunelle turned back to Kleinbart. "Does that make sense to you?"

"Not really," the doctor answered. "But I guess I'll just answer your questions."

"I'll take that," Brunelle answered. "Okay, first question. Doctor, does the report indicate whether there was any gunshot residue on Mr. Ostrander's hands?"

Kleinbart thumbed to the appropriate place in the report, read briefly to himself, then looked up. "Both of the decedent's hands were swabbed using the Modified Griess Test to detect any traces of nitrates. The presumptive test was negative."

Brunelle turned to Meckle. "Translation?"

But Meckle just offered wide eyes. "Uh, the gunshot residue test was negative?"

Brunelle rolled his eyes. "No. Translation: Peter Ostrander never fired his gun."

"I'm not sure I can say that," Kleinbart put it. "I can only say that the Modified Griess test was negative for nitrates."

"Exactly," Brunelle replied. "Which doesn't mean anything to the average juror. They don't care if your test was negative. They care if he shot his gun."

"I can't say that," Kleinbart protested. "I wasn't there. He might have been wearing gloves, or he might have washed his hands."

"I'm pretty sure he didn't wash his hands after he got shot in the head," Brunelle opined. "I don't think he took the time to remove his gloves after that either. I don't need you to say what happened out there. I just need you to say what the examination showed in here."

He pointed at Meckle. "And I need you to translate it into that story we need to tell the jury. Got it?"

Meckle nodded, more confidently. "I think so. Yes. Got it."

"Great. Let's try this again." Brunelle pointed at Kleinbart. "Was there any gunshot residue on Mr. Ostrander's hands?"

Kleinbart crossed his arms and frowned. But he answered the question. "No. The presumptive test was negative."

Brunelle pointed to Meckle.

"Mr. Ostrander never fired his gun," he said.

"Good, good." Brunelle smiled. "But from now on, call him 'Peter.'"

Meckle gave a thumbs-up. "Got it."

"Next question," Brunelle announced. "Was there any evidence of gunpowder stippling around the entrance wounds?"

Kleinbart looked down quickly at the autopsy report, but he knew the answer. "No."

"Translation?" Brunelle prompted Meckle.

"Peter wasn't shot up close," Meckle said.

"Say it differently," Brunelle encouraged. "Tell me what did happen, not what didn't."

Meckle considered for a moment. "Peter was shot from a distance."

"Exactly," Brunelle said. "So, was there a struggle for a gun or anything like that?"

"No, Peter was shot from a distance," Meckle answered. He was getting the hang of it. "The defendant shot Peter from across the parking lot before Peter ever even had a chance to get a shot off."

Brunelle smiled and nodded approvingly. But Kleinbart was uneasy.

"Now, wait a minute," the medical examiner interjected. "I never said anything even close to that. All I said was that there wasn't stippling around the wound. But you only see stippling if the shot is within about eighteen inches. The residual gunpowder that exits the barrel with the bullet doesn't travel any farther than that. And clothing can stop the gunpowder so that the skin around the wound could be free of stippling even if the shot was within eighteen inches."

"I'm sorry, doctor," Brunelle responded. "Wasn't there something about not drawing hypothetical conclusions from another expert's report?"

Kleinbart's expression hardened. "I think we're done. I really need to get back to work, Mr. Brunelle."

"Okay, one more question then," Brunelle insisted. "Were both of the gunshot wounds instantly fatal?"

Kleinbart took a moment. He might have wanted to end the interaction, but he did find the subject matter interesting. That's why he'd become a forensic pathologist in the first place. "The shot to the head certainly was. The one to the chest didn't strike the heart directly. It tore the aorta, but his heart would have beat for several more minutes, pumping blood into his chest cavity until there wasn't enough blood left in his veins to pump and he went into cardiac arrest."

"So, not fatal, but incapacitating," Brunelle confirmed.

"Correct."

Brunelle raised an eyebrow to Meckle.

The junior lawyer nodded. "The defendant shot Peter through the chest, incapacitating him, then delivered a kill shot directly between Peter's eyes. And that, ladies and gentlemen of the jury, is premeditated murder."

"Exactly." Brunelle nodded to his partner.

"But I didn't say that," Kleinbart protested.

"That's okay," Brunelle assured the doctor. "We'll say it for you."

CHAPTER 15

Meckle finished his brief and filed it, as required, a week before the hearing. There was other work to be done on other cases in that next week and soon enough Brunelle and Meckle found themselves in the courtroom of Judge Thomas H. Tillerson III. Judge Tillerson had recently been appointed to the Superior Court bench after over a decade as a District Court judge, presiding over misdemeanors and small claims. He was a prominent member of Seattle's African-American legal community and likely would have been appointed to the Superior Court bench sooner, except that he wanted to wait until his kids were all off to college and he would have the time necessary to devote to the serious cases that would come before him after the transition. It was a very responsible way to approach his career; and he expected the same level of responsibility from the advocates who appeared before him.

Brunelle wasn't sure he would quite live up to the judge's expectations. But he was pretty sure he'd come closer than Welles.

The case had been assigned to Tillerson for both motions and trial. Judge Tillerson didn't approve of the increasing practice of having one judge hear motions and another hear the trial. It might make cases move through the system faster, but how would the trial judge know whether to revisit an earlier ruling if he or she hadn't been the one to make that ruling, and to have heard the testimony and arguments upon which that ruling was based? No, when a case went to Judge Tillerson, it stayed with Judge Tillerson.

Brunelle and Meckle had arrived first, fifteen minutes before the hearing's scheduled time of 9:00 a.m. The corrections officers arrived a few minutes later, escorting the defendant from the jail and placing him securely in the defendant's chair to await the arrival of his attorney. He didn't have to wait too long. Welles arrived by 8:55, which was perfect. Enough time that they wouldn't get a late start, but not enough time for too much small talk before the judge took the bench. Brunelle didn't much like small talk. Not with Welles anyway.

"I read your response brief with great interest," Welles said to Brunelle after he'd checked in with his client and set his materials on the defense counsel table.

"Oh yeah?" Brunelle responded. "And what did you think?"

Welles frowned. "I didn't really enjoy it much, I must admit. But then again, I do prefer to read non-fiction."

Brunelle sighed. He wasn't interested in verbal jousting with Welles. It always felt like a waste of time and energy, even when it wasn't.

"Look," he said, "why don't we cut to the chase? Your guy is charged with Murder One, but I'll knock it down to Murder Two. Intentional murder instead of premeditated. It'll save him seven, maybe eight years. That's a good offer."

"It would be a good offer," Welles retorted, "if my client were guilty of murder. But he is guilty of nothing. He was defending himself, using lawful force, as provided for under the law. He is innocent."

"He's also looking at several decades in prison," Brunelle reminded him.

"Innocent people do not plead guilty," Welles declared.

"Okay. Well, I'm pretty sure that's not true," Brunelle answered. "Probably should be. But plenty of defendants take deals to avoid longer sentences after trial."

"Not my clients," Welles insisted. "I would never plead an innocent man to murder. And I am disappointed in you, my friend. I am disappointed."

Brunelle sighed again. "Fine." Then he leaned down and put a hand on Meckle's shoulder. "So, you wanna argue this?"

"This motion?" Meckle almost squeaked. "Uh, no. No, I think you should argue it. It's your case, Mr. Brunelle."

Brunelle raised a disapproving eyebrow at him.

"Dave," Meckle corrected himself. "It's your case, Dave."

"It's our case," Brunelle reminded him. "And it's your brief."

Before Meckle could protest any more, Judge Tillerson entered the courtroom.

"All rise!" the bailiff announced as he rose from his seat below the judge's bench. "The King County Superior Court is now in session, The Honorable Michael Tillerson III presiding."

Judge Tillerson took a beat to gaze down at the parties appearing before him. He was a tall man already, an impression only exaggerated by the raised dais of the judge's bench. He had graying temples and wrinkled, wise eyes behind large glasses. "Please be seated," he instructed.

Everyone complied. 'Everyone' meant the two lawyers, the defendant, the two corrections officers, and both court staff—bailiff and court reporter. Otherwise, the courtroom was empty, which was pretty typical for a preliminary motion hearing, even on an otherwise well-publicized murder case. Generally, the cameras showed up for the arraignment and the trial, but everything in between was too mundane or too complex for a compelling 30-second sound bite on the local news.

"This is the matter of the State of Washington versus Jeremy Huy Nguyen," Judge Tillerson announced for the record. "We are here for a hearing on the defense motion to dismiss pursuant to State versus Knapstad and progeny. Are the parties ready to proceed?"

Welles stood up first. It was his motion. "The defense is ready, Your Honor."

All eyes turned to the prosecution table. Brunelle gave Meckle an encouraging nudge, but the young lawyer shook his head tightly and pushed down in his seat.

Brunelle sighed and stood up to address the judge. "The State is ready, Your Honor."

Tillerson nodded approvingly. "All right then. This is a defense motion, so I will hear first from Mr. Welles."

"Thank you, Your Honor," Welles returned.

There were no witnesses for a Knapstad motion. The entire point was that the defense conceded—for the sake of the argument—everything the prosecution was alleging, but then argued that it still wasn't enough to establish a crime. It was all about oral advocacy. Talking. And Welles sure could talk. Brunelle settled in.

"The defendant's motion is, I believe, a matter of first impression in Washington courts," Welles began, "although, I must say, I was surprised, upon my initial research into the issue, to find there to be no precedent, published or otherwise, for the proposition put forth by the defense, since it seems so obvious and so definitive as to make dismissal of the case practically self-executing."

"Or perhaps," Judge Tillerson interrupted, "there's no precedent for your argument because it's so obviously flawed that no one else has had the temerity to bring it before a court."

"Temerity," Welles repeated, "or timidity? Or rather, the lack of timidity. And I challenge the Court also to avoid timidity, and show temerity. The temerity, the outright audacity, to hold the State to its burden, to require them to put forward evidence of every element of the crime charged, or else to dismiss the case."

"I understand your motion, Mr. Welles," the judge replied. "But I'm not sure I agree with your assertion that the State needs to put forward evidence which disproves a defense, so long as they put forward evidence of the statutory elements of the crime. In this case, the unlawful premeditated killing of another human being."

"I acknowledge your confusion, Your Honor," Welles began his response. Tillerson raised an eyebrow at the word 'confusion' but allowed

Welles to continue uninterrupted. "But allow me to educate the Court on the difference between statutory elements of a crime and non-statutory elements of a crime. Or rather in the lack of difference between those categories of elements."

"I don't need an education, Mr. Welles," the judge responded. "I need you to tell me why I should dismiss this case."

"You should dismiss it, Your Honor," Welles responded, "because the State cannot and will not be able to disprove self-defense beyond a reasonable doubt. Even if you assume the truth of all of the State's evidence to date, it still does not disprove self-defense. Lack of self-defense is a non-statutory element of the crime of murder. Duress, necessity, entrapment—those are affirmative defenses which a defendant must prove at trial. But self-defense is different. A defendant need not prove self-defense at trial; the State must disprove it, and disprove it beyond a reasonable doubt. They will be unable to do so here and so the case must be dismissed."

"But the State only has to do that if self-defense is somehow raised during the course of the trial," the judge returned. "They don't have to disprove it in every case, just in the cases where it's an issue."

"And it is absolutely an issue in this case," Welles returned.

"How so?" Judge Tillerson asked. "How is it raised in this case?"

"By my client, Your Honor," Welles seemed exasperated to have to say. "He himself told the detectives that he acted in self-defense."

"So, he admitted to the killing?" Tillerson asked.

"Uh, well, no, Your Honor," Welles answered. "Not in so many words. We still plan to hold the State to its burden of proving the standard, statutory elements of murder as well."

"Mm-hmm," Tillerson reacted. "And if I recall the briefing properly, the only thing your client said was, 'self-defense.' Nothing else. Just that."

"Correct, Your Honor," Welles confirmed.

Judge Tillerson looked over to Brunelle. "Do you plan to introduce that statement in your case-in-chief, Mr. Brunelle?"

Brunelle stood up. "Absolutely not, Your Honor."

"Yeah, I didn't think so," Tillerson said, almost to himself, as he turned back to Welles. "And you're not allowed to introduce it through the detectives because it's hearsay. If the jury is going to hear your client say it was self-defense, they're going to hear him say it from the witness stand, which will happen after the State rests its case-in-chief. So, if there's nothing in the State's evidence to support self-defense, why should I dismiss the case just because there's nothing to disprove it either?"

Welles exhaled and set his shoulders. "Regardless of whether the State introduces my client's statement or not, Mr. Nguyen still said it. Mr. Brunelle knows he said it, and Your Honor knows he said it. That means it's part of the truth of this case, and justice demands that the Court consider it."

"Justice demands?" Tillerson challenged. "If your client had confessed to the murder, but the confession was obtained illegally—no Miranda warnings, third degree, physical abuse—and there was no other evidence but that confession, would you be asking me to consider it? Would justice demand I consider an illegally obtained confession, even though it would be inadmissible at trial?"

"Of course not, Your Honor," Welles answered.

"So, what makes this different?" the judge demanded.

"It's different because we're the defense," Welles explained. "And the State is trying to put my client in a cage for the rest of his life. That means we garner every advantage and the State suffers every disadvantage. That is what the Constitution of this great nation demands. That is what justice demands. That, with all due respect, Your Honor, is what I demand."

Tillerson didn't respond immediately. Instead he chewed on his cheek and let his gaze linger on Welles even as he began to turn his head to Brunelle. Finally, he let his eyes catch up to his face and nodded toward the prosecutor. "Why is he wrong? Why shouldn't you have to put forward evidence at this stage to disprove self-defense, especially when the defendant himself raised the issue before charges were even filed?"

Brunelle took a moment before replying. He'd been around long enough and knew all the judges well enough to realize that Tillerson's argumentative tone with Welles didn't mean he agreed with the State; it just meant he liked to argue with the lawyers. And it was about to be Brunelle's turn. He wouldn't be able to add anything to the analysis Tillerson himself had used to bludgeon Welles. He shouldn't have to disprove it now because Nguyen couldn't raise it until after he'd rested his case. In theory, it might never be raised, and if it weren't, then he didn't have to disprove it. But that was a loser's argument. It was procedural, hiding behind evidence rules and courtroom protocols. But Welles was right: those rules were shields to protect criminal defendants, not swords to attack them. If he grabbed the hilt of that sword, it could turn to dust in his hand.

So, rather than hide behind why he didn't have to disprove self-defense, he stepped out from behind his table to explain how he would disprove it.

"In the early hours of a cold Seattle morning," he began, "the defendant, Jeremy Nguyen, saw Peter Ostrander standing alone in a parking lot. It was almost two a.m. in the International District and the bars would be emptying soon, their patrons heading home for the night. But for that brief time, Mr. Nguyen and Mr. Ostrander were the only people in the world, standing under the I-5 overpass, its never ceasing traffic drowning out the sounds of the rest of the world as two men faced each other, for the last time.

"But it wasn't the first time they'd met, or at least it wasn't the first time they'd come to know about each other. For you see, as often happens in cases of violence between young men, there was a young woman involved. A young woman who laid claim to both their hearts. A young woman named Joan, who had just given her name and number to Peter—or who had tried to. Peter was able to get her name, but only the first three digits of her phone number. They were interrupted. And they were interrupted by the defendant.

"Ms. Inha fled, but Peter stood his ground. Maybe he was unafraid. Maybe he was afraid, but stood his ground anyway, feeling some security in the handgun he carried on him. A handgun he hoped never to use. And one he never did use.

"But Mr. Nguyen had a handgun too. And he used it. He fired twice at Mr. Ostrander. The first shot pierced Peter's chest, tearing his aorta, his heart pumping blood into his chest cavity to crush his lungs as he bled to death. Then, intent on carrying out his plan for revenge, Jeremy Nguyen fired a second shot, aimed directly between Peter's eyes. A kill shot. An execution shot. Had there been any chance Peter might have survived that first shot to his chest, it was extinguished when Jeremy Nguyen's bullet pierced his skull and tore through his brain. He was dead before he hit the pavement.

"And that gun—the one he'd thought might protect him—it clattered from his hand, never fired. The defendant turned and fled, his plan carried out, his mission successful. But he was seen, and he was found, and he was arrested, and he was charged. And at the end of this case, he will be convicted of the murder he committed. A murder conceived in jealousy and executed in wrath. Murder, not self-defense. Never self-defense."

Brunelle looked up at the judge from his spot in the well between counsel tables and the bench. "Thank you, Your Honor."

Judge Tillerson was staring down at Brunelle, his head leaning on a hand. "Are you through?" he asked. "You know there's no jury here, right?"

Brunelle grinned slightly. "I know. But I also know that a jury should get to hear this case. It shouldn't be dismissed because the defense says the State can't prove something it has every intention of disproving. Killing a rival in a love triangle is not self-defense, Your Honor. And that's what the State intends to prove. The Court should deny the motion and let the case proceed to trial."

Tillerson's mouth screwed up into a knot as he considered what to do.

"May I be heard again, Your Honor?" Welles stood to ask. "I would be happy to preview my own opening statement, just like Mr. Brunelle, and explain why this is absolutely, one hundred percent, a self-defense case."

"I'm sure you would, Mr. Welles," Judge Tillerson half-laughed. "And I'm sure it would be twice as long and three times as eloquent as Mr. Brunelle's monologue. But I'm going to pass on that."

He sat up straight again to deliver his ruling. "Mr. Welles says the

State can't disprove self-defense beyond a reasonable doubt, so I should dismiss the case. Mr. Brunelle says not only can they disprove it, they will. But the key to this argument, in my estimation, is the word 'prove.' Proof is something that happens at trial, not here at a preliminary motion. This motion is premature."

"The reason for the preliminary motion, Your Honor," Welles implored, "is to avoid the necessity of an expensive and time-consuming trial when there can only be one possible result."

"You want me to dismiss a Murder One case?" Judge Tillerson asked. "Based on this motion?"

"Yes, Your Honor," Welles answered. "I do."

Judge Tillerson shook his head. "No way. If you want a dismissal, you'll have to get it from the jury."

Welles frowned. "Then it would be an acquittal, not a dismissal," he pointed out.

"Even better," Judge Tillerson observed. "Motion denied. Court is adjourned."

Tillerson left the courtroom just as quickly as he had entered it. When the door to his chambers closed, Welles stepped over to the prosecution table.

"An amazing story," he gushed. "But, as I said earlier, I prefer non-fiction. Where do you expect to find witnesses who will testify to that fairy tale of yours?"

"Well, I don't have the main witness," Brunelle answered, because your client killed him. But everything I said was a reasonable inference from the evidence we do have."

"Like what?" Welles challenged.

"Like the autopsy report, for one," Brunelle offered.

"The autopsy report?" Welles scoffed. "That examination was the definition of cursory. Just wait until I cross examine Dr. Delacourt about her methods, or lack thereof. The jury will know she did the bare minimum required to support your theory of the case and made no effort whatsoever to explore alternatives like self-defense."

"Uh, yeah, you might be waiting a while then." Brunelle rubbed the back of his neck. "We don't plan to call Dr. Delacourt. She's, uh, unavailable for this trial."

Welles's eyebrows knitted together, and he tipped his head ever so slightly. But rather than object, he simply asked, "Is that right? How do you plan to introduce the autopsy then?"

"Through Dr. Kleinbart," Meckle piped in. "He can testify from her report."

Welles nodded at the young prosecutor. "Right, right." The gears were clearly turning behind Welles's eyes. He changed topics slightly. "And this Joan Inha person? I haven't seen any witness statements from her. Does she even exist?"

"Why don't you ask your client?" Brunelle suggested. "I'm pretty sure he knows."

"Well, yes." Welles nodded and grinned slightly. "I'm pretty sure he does."

Welles nodded to Meckle, then reached out to shake Brunelle's hand. "Well played today, David. I shall see you again soon."

Too soon, Brunelle knew. Those gears had teeth.

CHAPTER 16

Brunelle knew the other shoe would drop. He just didn't know when. Which, he supposed, was the whole point of that metaphor. A man lying in bed in his thin-walled apartment, his upstairs neighbor arriving home from his late shift at the factory, ready to collapse into bed himself, pulling off a heavy work boot and dropping it on the floor. Then the wait for the next thud on the ceiling before either of them can go to sleep. A wait that lasted as long as it did, however long that might be. But eventually, that other shoe did drop.

He was sitting at his desk, checking his morning email, when Nicole came into his office, carrying the other shoe. Or an envelope with his name on it, anyway.

And the word 'PERSONAL' stamped on it.

So, it wasn't a brief from Welles.

It was a letter from Saint James.

Dear Mr. Brunelle:

This letter is in regard to the Human Resources complaint filed against you regarding allegation of sexual harassment.

The investigation has reached a point where we are ready to hear from you. We are requesting you submit to an interview by the Human Resources investigator assigned to this complaint. Failure to submit to the interview may result in repercussions on your employment status with the county.

We will contact you in the near future to schedule the interview and we expect your full and unreserved cooperation.

Sincerely,
Carmen Saint James
Chief Investigator
Human Resources Department

Brunelle closed his eyes as he pinched the bridge of his nose. He opened them again when his email pinged. A sidelong glance revealed an email from 'Human Resources' with the subject line 'Schedule Interview.' Brunelle didn't open it. Instead he stood up and walked into Duncan's office, without even knocking.

"Matt." He held up the envelope from Saint James. "I just got this letter from H.R. They want to interview me about that bogus complaint Delacourt filed. I'm furious."

Duncan looked up from whatever work Brunelle had interrupted. He could have castigated Brunelle for entering his office unannounced; they were friends, but he was still Brunelle's boss. Instead, he nodded and said, "Yeah, I understand."

"This is a bullshit witch hunt," Brunelle went on. "And we both know the first rule of talking with the cops—or any investigator—is don't."

Duncan nodded again. "Yeah, I understand."

"I mean, I don't have anything to hide," Brunelle defended, "but I don't trust them."

"I understand," Duncan answered.

Brunelle sighed and looked down again at the letter in his hand. "But

I have to do this, right? I mean, if I don't, then they only have her side of the story. And then I'm fucked."

Duncan shrugged. "I understand," he agreed.

"I just want this over with as soon as possible," Brunelle went on.

"I understand," Duncan empathized.

Brunelle stopped talking and considered his boss for several seconds. "I have to do this, don't I? Or else you get in trouble too?"

Duncan nodded and smiled. "And now you understand."

Brunelle dropped himself into one of Duncan's guest chairs. "Fuck, Matt. I don't want to do this. I'm gonna say something stupid."

But Duncan was ready with his usual sage advice. "No, you won't. Just tell the truth. The truth is never stupid."

But Brunelle just shook his head and grinned sardonically. "Oh, Matt. I thought you understood."

CHAPTER 17

"Thank you for taking the time to sit down with me, Mr. Brunelle."

The interview with Human Resources was scheduled for 4:00 p.m. the following Monday. The sooner the better, Brunelle figured. If he was going to get screwed, he might as well get it over with. And if he wasn't, well, then, he had work to do.

For better or worse, the investigator was not Carmen Saint James. Instead it was an equally stern-faced woman named Linda Guillen. Brunelle had hoped they might send a man, although he supposed if they had, it would have been for the purpose of getting Brunelle to relax, maybe 'bro it up' and admit to the alleged misconduct, write it off stupidly as 'locker room talk' or some equally lame, and inculpatory, excuse.

Guillen had thick black curls pulled back into a tightly managed ponytail. She was younger than Brunelle and dressed sharper too, with a dark business suit over a cream blouse. She also seemed a lot more at ease about the entire situation than Brunelle was. More in control anyway, which Brunelle supposed was accurate.

"Let's get right to it, shall we?" Guillen began from her spot at the head of the conference table, the view of Mount Rainier to her left. Well, it would have been a view of Mount Rainier if it had been a clearer day. Instead it was a view of the southern end of Elliott Bay and Beacon Hill, past which, on clear days, Mount Rainier was often visible. She opened her laptop and readied her fingers over the keyboard. "You know why I'm here today, correct? You're aware of the allegations against you?"

Brunelle nodded. "Yes, I'm aware."

"Good," Guillen answered, her fingers still hovering over the keys. "So, I won't bother restating them. Would you like to tell me your side of the story?"

"Does it matter?" Brunelle inquired with a shrug.

Guillen raised an eyebrow at him. "Does it matter?" she parroted. "I'm here for a reason, Mr. Brunelle. I'm not in the habit of wasting other people's time. And I'm certainly not in the habit of wasting my own. This is a serious allegation about a serious issue and it merits a serious response. I had hoped you'd be more cooperative, although I can't say I'm surprised by your attitude."

"No, what I meant was," Brunelle clarified, "does it matter if I say it again or if you already heard it all from Dr. Delacourt?"

Guillen frowned. "I don't understand."

"I'm not contesting the facts of the allegation," Brunelle explained. "But I disagree with how they've been interpreted."

"You called a county employee with over twenty-one years of formal education a 'girl,'" Guillen reminded him.

"I called a person who I thought was an ex-girlfriend a 'girl,'" Brunelle defended, "using a quote from a movie."

"What movie?" Guillen asked.

Brunelle didn't actually know. "Uh, I'm not sure. It's just that, 'What's a nice girl like you doing in a place like this?' quote. Maybe 'Casablanca'?"

Guillen shook her head at him. "It's the title of a 1963 short film by Martin Scorsese."

"It is?" Brunelle asked.

"It is," Guillen confirmed. "At least get your references straight."

"Sorry," Brunelle apologized. "I just, well, I was trying to be funny. I guess maybe I could have updated the word 'girl.'"

"It's not 1963 anymore, Mr. Brunelle," Guillen pointed out.

"I know that," he agreed.

"There's plenty of other language from that time," she went on, "that I'm sure you wouldn't use. Language used to describe other people. Discriminatory, denigrating language that doesn't deserve ever to be spoken."

"Well, 'girl' is still an actual word," Brunelle pointed out. "I mean, a young female human is a girl."

"And an adult female with multiple degrees is not," Guillen shot back. "Is that understood?"

It wasn't going well. Brunelle's plan had been to avoid talking about the actual incident and instead argue that it didn't amount to sexual harassment, or gender harassment, or whatever it was he was accused of exactly. But now that he was in the middle of that fight, he wasn't getting anywhere with it. If anything, he was losing ground. So, he tried another tack.

"I understand," he said.

"You understand?" Guillen repeated back.

"Yes, I understand now," Brunelle confirmed. "And I'm sorry."

"You're sorry?" Guillen echoed, her tone dripping with incredulity.

"Yes, I'm sorry."

Brunelle had learned a long time ago not to fight losing battles. You still lost them, but you also damaged your credibility for future battles. If a piece of evidence wasn't coming in, concede that and move on. If you wasted everyone's time arguing for a result that was clearly unsupported by the facts and the law, then you gained a reputation as a hack, an advocate who would argue anything for his side. But if you conceded that an adverse result was required by the law, then you gained a reputation as someone who was fair and whose judgment could be trusted. He could tell he wasn't going to convince Linda Guillen that his little joke was okay. So, he might as well concede it wasn't and express his remorse. That would also avoid discussing the facts of the case, at least directly.

"What are you sorry for?" Guillen tested. She still hadn't typed anything into her computer. Her hands had lowered onto the conference table about the time she cited the Scorsese short.

"I'm sorry I used a term that offended someone else," Brunelle answered. "I'm sorry I didn't realize it would offend that someone else. And I'm sorry that it's come to this."

Guillen frowned at that last part. "So, you're sorry you got caught?"

Brunelle could sympathize with the sentiment. He'd had it himself regarding defendants he was prosecuting, more times than he could count. "No, I'm just sorry. Please tell Dr. Delacourt that I'm sorry."

Guillen took several moments to think, while Brunelle sat uneasily in his chair. He looked out the window again to see if maybe the mountain had come out after all. But no.

Guillen closed her laptop with a loud click. "Thank you, Mr. Brunelle. I think I have what I came for. We are almost finished with our investigation, after which there will be recommendations. I can tell you this, there will likely be discipline in a case like this. This isn't the sort of thing that the county can just turn a blind eye to. Not now. Not any more."

"I understand," Brunelle repeated. "It was meant to be a joke. But it wasn't funny, and I shouldn't have said it. I understand that now."

Guillen's face twisted with contemplation. "You know," she confided, "I wasn't really prepared for this. I expected a long, drawn-out interview, where you attempted to dodge my questions, spin your answers, and blame the victim. You realize you could be terminated for this sort of behavior?"

Brunelle wasn't sure that was quite true. It was a joke—a bad joke, but a joke nonetheless. If he were terminated for one joke in a 20-year career, the county might have another complaint on their hand—a wrongful termination lawsuit. But instead of saying any of that, Brunelle offered another, "I understand."

"But your conciliation is refreshing." Guillen offered as she stood up to leave, "even if likely calculated. We will consider it when making our recommendation."

"Uh, great." Brunelle stood up as well. He extended a hand.

But Guillen ignored it. "Goodbye, Mr. Brunelle. I'll see myself out."

CHAPTER 18

As soon as the interview with Guillen was over, Brunelle skipped going back to his own office and instead went directly downstairs.

"I need a drink," he announced when he reached Carlisle's office.

Carlisle looked up from her desk. "At 4:50 on a Monday?"

"Yes."

"Awesome," Carlisle laughed. "I know just the place."

* * *

The place was, in fact, named 'The Place.' It was just past the Pioneer Square district, where most of the lawyers and courthouse staffers could be expected to congregate after work, but not quite to the International District where Brunelle had searched in vain for the mysterious Miss Inha.

It was half bar, half pool hall, almost literally. On one side was a long, shiny, well-stocked cocktail bar with two bartenders and already several patrons who'd beaten them to the first round of mixed drinks. On the other were six pool tables, two of which already hosted games between beer-drinking friends. Brunelle looked side to side, but knew he'd enjoy a game of pool a hell of a lot more after he had a good, stiff drink in him. Maybe two. Definitely two.

"So, rough day?" Carlisle asked after they'd placed their orders with one of the bartenders. Brunelle got a Manhattan; Carlisle went with a gin and tonic.

Brunelle shrugged. "Tough end of the day. I got interviewed by some H.R. investigator about that complaint the M.E. filed."

"About that stupid joke?" Carlisle confirmed. "Did you tell him it wasn't even funny?"

"Her," Brunelle corrected. "And no, that didn't seem to be a viable defense."

"So, what did you go with?"

The bartender set their drinks down in front of them.

Brunelle picked up his and took a sip. "I went with 'I'm sorry.'"

"You copped to it?" Carlisle nearly spit her drink out. "Why would you do that? You should have lawyered up. You should always lawyer up."

"It's not an actual criminal case," Brunelle protested. "I'm not looking at jail time."

"You're looking at losing your job, though," Carlisle pointed out.

Another shrug from Brunelle. "Maybe. But probably more so if I don't cooperate. And definitely more if I lie. I actually have less protection than a criminal defendant. That whole right to remain silent thing only applies to criminal procedure, not employment issues."

"Are you sure about that?" Carlisle asked over another sip of gin.

Brunelle thought for a moment, then laughed. "No." He shook his head. "But I think it may have worked. The investigator seemed surprised. I didn't actually talk about the facts. I just said I was sorry. She didn't seem to know what to do with that."

"Well, I wouldn't get your hopes up," Carlisle cautioned. "Women are hard to read."

Brunelle was about to point out that was exactly the sort of comment that should get someone in trouble with H.R., but before he could say anything, a woman's voice called out from behind him.

"Dave? Dave the Narc? Is that you?"

Brunelle turned around to see the woman from the restaurant line. Abbie... Something.

"Abbie, right?" he ventured. "Nice to see you again."

And it was, in part because she was nice to see. Her thick blonde curls still hung loosely around the base of her neck, and she was wearing a tank top which confirmed Brunelle's earlier suspicions that the tattoo on her neck was connected to the one on her arm. It was one continuous illustration featuring what appeared to be several pink dolphins. Below the tank top was a pair of sweatpants that were loose-fitting but still managed somehow to highlight her feminine curves.

"Who's this?" Abbie pointed to Carlisle. "Narckette?" Then, more genuinely, she added, "Seriously, though, nice suit."

"Gwen," Carlisle introduced herself with a small wave. "And thanks. I got it off this great website that does custom suits for super cheap."

"Oh, I would totally look into that," Abbie said, "except I never wear suits."

Carlisle looked at Brunelle, but he just shrugged. He barely knew Abbie either.

"Speaking of which," Abbie put her hands on her hips and cocked her head at them, "isn't it a little early on a Monday for a couple of narcs to be drinking?" Then her eyebrows shot up. "Oh, unless this is a date. Oh wow, is this a date?"

Carlisle laughed at that. "Oh, no. Definitely not."

Brunelle frowned at her. "Definitely not? Why definitely not?"

Carlisle smirked knowingly at him. "You're not my type."

"Good," Abbie said, grabbing Brunelle's arm and pulling him off his stool. "Come on, you two. Play pool with us. We need another team."

'Good?' Brunelle mouthed at Carlisle as Abbie pulled him toward the pool tables.

Carlisle shrugged. "Maybe she was talking about me," she whispered back. "I told you. Women are hard to read. May the best narc win."

The rest of Abbie's crew was decidedly non-narc-like. Three men and two other women, all of them wore some variation of her outfit: tank top or T-shirt, sweatpants or shorts or martial arts pants. Most of the shirts had the silhouette of someone kicking a lot higher than Brunelle could ever have hoped to raise his leg, even in his heyday.

"These are some of my friends from the capoeira studio where I teach," Abbie explained. Sort of.

"Cap-what-uh?" Brunelle asked.

Abbie and Carlisle both frowned at him disapprovingly. Abbie for not knowing what capoeira was; Carlisle for admitting as much.

"Capoeira," Abbie repeated. "It's a Brazilian martial art. I'm one of the instructors at our studio."

"Is that where you said you work?" Brunelle remembered. "The place in the International District?"

Abbie grinned at him. "I didn't say where I worked."

"You said you worked in the I.D.," Brunelle reminded her. "And then pointed to roughly where the body was found."

"Body?" Abbie's eyes flew wide.

But before either of the narcs could respond, one of Abbie's associates, a tall man with natty hair and caramel skin, called out in an accented voice, "Hey, Boto! Who are your friends?"

"Pintado!" Abbie yelled back. "This is Narc and Narckette." She gestured from Brunelle and Carlisle to her group. "Narc and Narckette, this is Pintado, Aguaviva, Urso, Tartaruga, and Girafa."

Brunelle waved at the group. "It's Dave actually, not Narc."

"My name really is Narckette," Carlisle deadpanned.

Brunelle turned his attention back to Abbie. "Boto?" he asked.

Abbie grinned and nodded. "That's my capoeira name." She pointed at the cetaceans swimming up her arms. "Botos are pink dolphins that live in the Amazon River. Everyone gets a Portuguese capoeira name when they join a studio."

Brunelle looked to Pintado. "So, your real name isn't Pintado?"

Pintado shrugged. "Who's to say what name is real? When I'm with my people here, I am Pintado, the tiger fish."

"And when he's not Pintado," Abbie went ahead and sated Brunelle's curiosity, "his name is Luiz. He's from Brazil. Just like Urso and Tartaruga. They're up visiting for our *batizado*."

Brunelle started to ask, so Abbie answered that question too. "It's a big annual festival put on by every studio. Our *professor* is affiliated with a studio in Rio, so our *mestre* and some of his *formados* came up from Brazil."

Brunelle nodded for several seconds, waiting to comprehend. Then he decided he didn't need to understand. He took another drink from his glass. "So, we're playing pool?"

Abbie laughed. "Yeah, we were going to play three to a side, but that's no fun. We'll grab two tables and split into groups. You and Narckette can play against me and Pintado."

"It's Gwen," Brunelle felt compelled to correct Abbie.

"No, it's Narckette," Carlisle insisted. "It's my capoeira pool name."

Brunelle rolled his eyes, but then he grabbed a pool cue off the wall. "Loser buys the drinks, right, Boto?"

Abbie smiled broadly as she grabbed her own cue. "Of course, Narc."

* * *

Thirty minutes later, there was one striped ball, two solids, and the 8-ball left. Brunelle and Carlisle were stripes, and it was Brunelle's turn.

"Why don't we make this a little more interesting?" he suggested as he lined up his shot—a difficult carom around the 8- and 2-balls. "If you win, you still buy the drinks, but if we win we get tickets to your batman-zah-po."

"Batizado," Abbie corrected with a giggle.

"What did I say?" Brunelle joked.

"There are no tickets," Pintado said from his spot on a stool across the pool table.

"Uh, yeah," Abbie interjected. "Totally sold out. But, uh, let's see…"

"What about some type of VIP pass?" Brunelle pushed on. "A backstage pass or something?"

Abbie grinned, first at Pintado then at Brunelle. "Sure. VIP backstage passes. You got it. But free drinks for us if we win. Deal?"

Brunelle nodded. "Deal." Then he leaned down and took the shot. He missed. The cue ball hit the 12-ball, but the 12 didn't even come close to the pocket.

Pintado took the next shot in silence, also missing his opportunity to sink the 2-ball. But he set up Carlisle perfectly. She tapped in the 12, then called the final shot and sank the 8-ball in the far corner pocket.

"Game, Narc and Narckette," she announced. "Although, now I wish we'd stuck with the original bet. My drink is empty."

Pintado laughed. "Yeah, and we don't sell tickets to a batizado. It's free. Anyone can come."

Carlisle dropped her head at Brunelle. "You idiot. We just lost out on free drinks."

Brunelle looked at Abbie. "You lied to us?"

"I lied to you," Abbie corrected. "Narckette wasn't the one trying to change the bet. And anyway, I didn't lie about everything." She offered a coy smile. "If you do come to the batizado, Dave, I can still give you the VIP treatment."

That sounded good to Brunelle. Carlisle huffed, then laughed, then headed back to the bar with her empty glass. "This round's on you, *Daaave*," she called out over her shoulder.

Brunelle smiled, but didn't take his eyes off Abbie. "Deal."

CHAPTER 19

The thing about shoes dropping was, there were never really just two shoes. Not for most people, and certainly not for a homicide prosecutor. There wasn't just one factory worker living upstairs; it was his whole crew, with so many shoes dropping it was easy to lose track if there were any more to drop. And while Brunelle might not have known exactly how many workers were dropping shoes on his ceiling at any given time, he knew at least two of the workers were named Welles and Guillen. And he knew they hadn't finished taking off their shoes just yet.

In fact, sometimes two shoes dropped at the same time. But sometimes it didn't even matter, because the rest of the day—or the previous night—was so good.

"Mail call!" Nicole called out to Brunelle as he turned the corner to his office the next morning. "And nothing good."

Brunelle diverted to Nicole's desk. "You don't know that," he disagreed as he took the two items she was holding out for him. "Let's see what these say."

The first was a brief, delivered that morning by legal messenger from the Law Office of William Harrison Welles. "Defendant's Motion to Exclude Testimony of Dr. Eric Kleinbart," Brunelle read the caption aloud. "Right on schedule."

"You don't think that's a problem," Nicole gestured toward the other piece of mail she'd handed him, "given your other situation?"

"Let's find out." He tore open the sealed envelope from County Human Resources, with the initials 'L.G.' handwritten under the return address. "Dear Mr. Brunelle," he began, "We have concluded the initial investigation of this matter... blah, blah, blah... take these sorts of allegations very seriously... blah, blah, blah... Ah, here we are: 'It is our recommendation that you attend a sensitivity training course to educate you on the topics of... blah, blah, blah... More blah... Ah, and if you successfully complete the course, the matter will be closed. If you choose to ignore this recommendation or appeal, blah, blah, blah... Yours in perpetual malice, Linda Guillen.'"

"That's not how she signed it," Nicole said.

Brunelle shrugged. "Yeah, I dunno. I was skimming."

Nicole giggled and shook her head. "Sensitivity training? That is awesome. Couldn't happen to a nicer guy. Can I come?"

"I don't think it's a 'plus one' situation," Brunelle guessed.

"No ask, no get," Nicole argued.

"If I ask Linda Guillen if I can bring a date to my sensitivity training class, I'm guessing I'll get fired."

Nicole feigned a blush and fanned herself with her hand. "A date? Why, Mr. Brunelle, you presume too much, I think."

"See?" Brunelle replied. "This is why I can't take you."

"Because I'm hilarious?"

Brunelle smiled. "Sure."

"So, does that impact Welles's motion at all?" Nicole asked. "I mean, if the H.R. thing is over..."

Brunelle considered. "Probably. Maybe. If I cared."

"You don't care?" Nicole sounded concerned.

"Not really."

"Why not?"

"Because first," Brunelle explained, "Delacourt is the better witness anyway. And second, I just got a real date, with a lovely young woman I beat at pool last night."

"Wait. You had to win a bet to get a date with her?" Nicole asked.

Brunelle paused. "I hadn't thought of it that way."

"Don't worry," Nicole laughed. "I'm sure she has."

CHAPTER 20

There was at least one more shoe Brunelle was waiting to hear drop. Not just waiting, hoping. And not just a shoe, a boot. A huge boot. Like an astronaut's boot. Unless those were made out of some super-advanced lightweight material. Maybe those metal boots the deep-sea divers wore to walk on the bottom of the ocean, with the big round brass helmet with the windows and the hose that went back up to a boat on the surface. *Did people still do that?* he wondered, although not enough to Google it.

In any event, that big, heavy, astronaut/diver boot was named Joan Inha. And the worker who needed to drop it on Brunelle's ceiling already was named Larry Chen.

Brunelle took care of matters in his in-box that morning, then made plans to corner Chen in his office after lunch. But best laid plans...

"Chen's out in the field," Montero informed Brunelle after he'd made it past the officer guarding the entrance from his receptionist's desk in the lobby. "Working on a lead."

"On my case?" Brunelle asked hopefully. "The shooting in the International District?"

Montero's mouth twisted into a knot as she considered, but then she shook her head. "I don't think so. I think it was one of his cold cases. He's down at the Jungle, trying to find some homeless guy who might have seen something, like, ten years ago."

"Sounds promising," Brunelle wisecracked. "The Jungle, huh?"

"Yeah." Then Montero looked concerned. "You're not thinking about going down there yourself, are you?"

"Actually, I was," Brunelle admitted.

"You want me to come with you?" Montero offered, her hand moving vaguely toward her holster.

"I think I'll be okay," Brunelle assured her. Although he wasn't certain, given her reaction.

Montero looked Brunelle up and down. "Well, at least lose the tie. Nobody wears suits any more. They'll think you're a narc. And you don't want those guys thinking you're a narc."

* * *

Heeding Montero's advice, Brunelle actually took the time to swing by his condo and change fully from his suit and tie into jeans and sneakers. Partially because he was tired of being called a narc, but mostly because the Jungle didn't feature sidewalks and he didn't want to ruin his loafers in the mud—and whatever else—he was going to step in. And he figured he was going to step in it, one way or another.

The main entrance—to the extent any of the myriad ways of slipping into and out of the homeless camp could be described as a *main* entrance—was off South Dearborn Street. This particular version of the Jungle was sometimes referred to as Jungle 3.0. Jungle 1.0 had existed, in one form or another, for some eighty years, beginning as a 'hobo jungle' on the steep hillside of Beacon Hill, south of Downtown. It survived the growth and expansion of the city, reacting to the addition of the interstate by sliding itself under the protective, if cacophonous, overpass built over the hillside, barely tall enough for a grown man to stand under. But after a particularly newsworthy triple murder, the city leaders couldn't ignore the Jungle any more and rousted the residents. Some found more stable housing, some left for other cities, but most resettled nearby, under a different overpass, and started Jungle 2.0. But home is home, and eventually people made their way back to the original location of Seattle's largest and longest running shantytown and started Jungle 3.0.

The latest grown man to stand, his head only inches below the vibrating concrete of Interstate-5, was a local district attorney whose job—or part of it—had been to trade these people's homes from a tent city under a freeway to a jail cell for whatever substances and violence they eventually visited upon themselves and others.

But not that day. That day, he was only interested in a crime that had happened weeks earlier under a different section of that interstate. And in finding the detective who was, in theory anyway, supposed to be helping him hold responsible the culprit who had committed that crime.

There was a wide muddy path that quickly gave way to a maze of tents, cardboard sleeping mats, and half packed bags of belongings. Even though it was the middle of the afternoon, a lot of those tents and mats and bags had people sleeping in or on them. What people who were awake huddled around each other, some staring at the obvious interloper in their midst, others in no state to notice much more than whatever sensations were overwhelming their brains right then.

Brunelle's own brain was feeling a little overwhelmed itself. He was so far out of his element, he might as well have been on another planet. He kept his gaze down, in part to avoid eye contact with anyone, in part not to step on anyone or anything as he made his way deeper into the Jungle. It was the middle of the afternoon, but it still seemed darker in there somehow, and the stench of so many people living so close together with so little sanitation was nothing less than oppressive—in more ways than one, Brunelle considered.

"Hey!" shouted someone behind him. A man. An angry man with a raspy voice.

Brunelle ignored him, but looked up a little to speed his way deeper into the Jungle, and farther from the voice.

"Hey!" the man yelled again. "Hey! Who are you? What are you doing here? You don't belong here!"

Brunelle could hardly argue with that. But he couldn't ignore the man either—even if only because that would have been unsafe. You don't keep your back turned to a stranger who's yelling at you. You turn around and size him up. Brunelle stopped and did just that. He was hoping for an emaciated heroin addict, maybe an elderly alcoholic. Someone he could take without falling into the mud and feces and needles under his feet.

No such luck.

It was a short, thick man, probably in his 30s, with a grizzled beard and dirty hands. He'd probably been in more fist fights that morning than Brunelle had been in his entire life.

"Look, man." Brunelle raised his hands to him like a bank robber encountering a line of cops with their guns leveled. "I'm not looking for any trouble. I'm just trying to find a friend."

The man laughed. "You got friends here?"

"Maybe," Brunelle answered. "I mean, he's supposed to be here. Tall guy. Chinese."

The man's scowl softened. "Larry? You're friends with Larry?"

"Larry?" Brunelle repeated. Nobody called Chen 'Larry.' Except his wife, maybe. But he was on a first name basis with one of the Jungle's self-appointed enforcers? Brunelle wondered what this guy would think if he knew his pal 'Larry' was a cop. "Uh, yeah," Brunelle confirmed. "Larry and I are friends."

"You a cop too?" the man asked.

Okay, they know he's a cop.

"Uh, not exactly," Brunelle deflected, before repeating his question, "Is he here?"

The man didn't answer immediately. Instead, he just stared at Brunelle, his gaze hardening and the scowl returning. "Larry always comes alone. I don't think you're his friend. I don't think you should be here." He shook his head as he settled into his conclusion. "You shouldn't be here."

Shit, Brunelle thought. He wasn't going to win a physical fight with this guy. Not easily anyway. But he didn't think his verbal jousting skills were likely to carry the day either. They probably wouldn't even carry the next minute.

"Look, man," he said again, as if maybe the familiarity of the expression might convince this total stranger not to attack him. "I can leave. I can talk to Larry later. No big deal. Really."

"I don't know," the man growled. "It seems like a big deal to me. You don't belong here."

"Then I'll leave," Brunelle offered. He took a step back, but that was actually the wrong direction, deeper into the Jungle. The angry man was blocking the way he'd come.

"Oh, you'll leave, all right," the man agreed. "But not until I make sure you never come back."

The next few seconds were a blur as time seemed to both slow and speed up at the same time. The man lowered his shoulders and started at Brunelle at a full sprint. Brunelle stepped back into the mud to brace himself against the coming tackle. Then someone else grabbed him from behind, but rather than pulling him down, the hand on the collar of his shirt stood him up straight and held him steady.

"Michael!" Chen boomed as he stepped out in front of Brunelle. "Stop!"

'Michael' came to a stuttering, muddy halt only a few feet before he would have knocked down both Brunelle and his newly appeared guardian angel.

"Larry?" Michael's eyes flew wide in deep-set sockets. "This guy says he knows you. He, he was looking for you. But I didn't think he really knew you. I, I—"

"He knows me," Chen assured Michael. His voice was as calm and forceful as his stance. Brunelle forgot sometimes just what a large man Chen was. He was always so unassuming and soft-spoken, he seemed more teddy bear than grizzly bear.

But the grizzly bear was there too. He turned to Brunelle. "What the hell are you doing here?" he demanded. "You don't belong here."

"And you do?" was Brunelle's instinctive response. A mistake, he knew as soon as he said it.

"More than you," Chen rumbled. "These people know me. They trust me. When I come here, it's not to bust them for drugs or run them for warrants. I'm here to help them."

Brunelle was still flush with the adrenaline of almost being attacked. And he was still mad at Chen for not working harder on his case. He threw his arms wide and looked around at the squalor that surrounded them. "You're doing a hell of a job."

"Why are you here?" Chen repeated his demand.

"I needed to talk to you," Brunelle answered. "Montero said you were here."

"What's so important it couldn't wait until I was done here?"

"What's so important here," Brunelle returned fire, "that it couldn't wait until you'd found Joan Inha?"

"That's why you're here?" Chen barked. "That stupid Joan Inha lead? You came all the way out here to see if I'd found your stupid motive witness?"

"She's not a stupid motive witness," Brunelle shot back. "She's the key to the whole case. But you're out here spending the day with Michael and Sally and whoever else in the Jungle, when you claim you don't have time to go to the International District and ask a few questions to track down the one witness who can put this entire case together for the jury."

Chen took a beat, then crossed his arms. "Do you want to know why I'm here, Dave?"

"Yes," Brunelle snapped. "Yes, I do."

"I'm here because of Elaine Schillinger," Chen answered.

"I, I don't know who that is," Brunelle said after a moment.

"She was a drug addict," Chen expounded. "And a prostitute. And a mother. She was forty-two years old; she was homeless; and she lived here, in the Jungle. Until some bastard shot her in the face five blocks from here."

"When did that happen?" Brunelle asked. "I didn't hear anything about a murder around here this week."

"It happened nine years ago, Dave," Chen told him. "Nine years ago. Some piece of shit picked her up from here, drove her to a secluded alleyway for a blow job, then decided it would be more fun to put a bullet through her face. No sex. There was no DNA. No witnesses, either. Just neighbors who heard the shot and looked out the window to see the taillights of a car driving away. He just left her on the side of the road, like a bag of garbage. The M.E. said it probably took her three to five minutes to bleed out. By the time aid arrived, she was gone.

"That was nine years ago. Never solved. It got assigned to some detective who was two months from retirement. I knew him. He was good, once, back in the day. But he was two months from retirement. He interviewed a few people. They confirmed she said she was going out to hook so she could get enough money for food and drugs that day. But there were no obvious leads, and he didn't make any effort to develop new ones. The case went cold. Never closed, because it was never solved, but it went cold. Just sat in a storeroom of file boxes until I started opening those up.

"Whoever did it, Dave, he's still out there. He thinks he got away with it. But he's not gonna. Not if I have anything to say about it. And that's why I'm here."

Brunelle took a few moments to reply. Of course he cared about this other case. But it was still another case. Not the one hanging in front of his face right then.

"What makes her case more important than my case?" he demanded.

"Your case is solved," Chen answered. "You know who did it. That murderer has been arrested. He's sitting in jail awaiting trial."

"A trial I can't win without Joan Inha," Brunelle returned. "It's not enough to know who did it. We have to hold him responsible. I'm asking you to help me hold him responsible."

But Chen just frowned and shook his head. "How do you know she'll help you? How do you know she won't help Nguyen? You've got a nice clean case, Dave. Your victim was shot twice, including right between the eyes. He never fired his gun. Nguyen can cry self-defense all day, but the jury won't believe him. He's the freaking defendant—of course they won't believe him. Unless, Joan Inha takes the witness stand and corroborates his story. Maybe just leave well enough alone. Go forward with what you have. Why do you want more if you don't know for sure the more will help you?"

It was a fair question. But Brunelle knew the answer to it.

"I want to know the truth," he said. "All of it, good and bad. If it was self-defense, I want to know that too. You're right. The jury won't believe Nguyen. I don't believe him either. But if we can find Joan Inha and she says it was self-defense… Well, I don't want to prosecute an innocent man."

Chen laughed. "No one's innocent, Dave. You know that. I don't care if you call it murder or self-defense, Nguyen killed that guy. And someone killed Elaine Schillinger when she was using drugs and prostituting."

Chen shook his head at Brunelle. "You don't belong here, Dave. Go home, put your suit back on, and take care of the cases I've already solved for you. Let me do my job and maybe I can give you one more."

Brunelle didn't know how to respond. So he didn't. He turned and walked away, through the mud and shit, past Michael and his stench, back to the world he thought he probably still knew.

CHAPTER 21

That world Brunelle knew was populated with lawyers and legal assistants, judges and court reporters. Cops too, to be sure, but at a distance. Similar, but not the same. It was good to be reminded of that sometimes.

One of those lawyers was his co-counsel, Mr. Gregory Meckle. And even though nine out of ten times, Brunelle would have preferred the company of a cop like Chen over a lawyer like Meckle, there was work to do. Lawyer work.

"Hey, Gregory," Brunelle greeted his second-chair as he entered Meckle's office uninvited. "Got a minute?"

Meckle spun away from his computer monitor. "For you. Mr. Bru—I mean, Dave? Of course. Always."

"Good," Brunelle replied and he dropped himself into one of Meckle's guest chairs. He tossed Welles's motion to exclude Kleinbart on Meckle's desk. "I need a response to this. You up to writing it?"

"Of course," Meckle answered eagerly. Then he picked it up. "Uh, what is it?"

"Welles wants to prevent Kleinbart from testifying from Delacourt's report," Brunelle explained. "He wants us to call Delacourt. The thrust of his argument is that it's a Confrontation Clause problem if he can't cross-examine the actual pathologist who conducted the autopsy, especially when we're relying on the results of the autopsy to argue inferences against self-defense."

Meckle thought for a few moments. "That sounds like a pretty good argument."

"It is," Brunelle agreed. "See if you can make a better one."

He stood up to leave. There was no need for further explanation, and part of his world or not, Meckle wasn't someone he wanted to make small talk with. He really didn't care how his weekend was.

"Uh, Dave?" Meckle called out after him as he reached the door. "When do you need this done by?"

"How soon can you do it?" Brunelle asked. Then, before Meckle could actually answer, "That's when I need it done by."

"Okay," Meckle acknowledged. "I'll get it to you as soon as I can."

But Brunelle shook his head. "I don't need to review it. Just give it to Nicole to file. You can sign it. It's your response."

"But it's your case," Meckle protested.

Brunelle considered the polite response, namely, 'No, Gregory, it's our case.' But instead he opted for honesty. "Yes, it is." Then he left.

Carlisle happened to be right outside Meckle's office. She had some papers in her hand; it looked like she was on her way to the copier.

"You're going to let him file a brief you haven't even reviewed?" she questioned him. Then, almost as an afterthought, "I was eavesdropping, by the way."

Brunelle acknowledged the eavesdropping part with a simple nod, then answered her question. "Yes, I am."

"Do you think that's smart?"

Brunelle smiled. "I think it's brilliant."

CHAPTER 22

Brunelle spent the next several days safely in his known world. He relaxed. He recharged. And he considered what his similar, not quite the same, detective friend said about whether he really wanted to find Joan Inha or not. Then, once relaxed and recharged, it was time to venture outside of his world again to someone else's. But it was someone who he was hoping might become a part of his world too, at least for a little while.

Brunelle hadn't been to Abbie's capoeira studio before, but the address was readily available online. He expected it to look like any other martial arts dojo he'd seen: a store front in a strip mall, with a floor-to-ceiling mirror and wall-to-wall mats, maybe some awards and trophies displayed somewhere near the entrance.

Instead, near as Brunelle could tell, the 'studio' was an abandoned garage. A large, commercial mechanic's garage to be sure, but a garage nonetheless. There were no mats on the floor, just oil stains. And the only decoration was a full-wall mural of several silhouetted *capoeiristas* showing off their skills in front of a rolling wave of rainbows and Brazilian flags. It reminded Brunelle of the T-shirts Abbie and her friends had been wearing at the pool hall, only much, much larger.

In fact, the figures on the mural were at least ten feet tall, rising up to the vaulted ceiling of the two-story tall garage. It would have been difficult to see them otherwise, because by the time Brunelle arrived the garage/studio was packed, wall-to-painted-wall with people. There were more capoeiristas than he could count. Most of the men wore just white pants and no shirts, while the women wore white pants and tank tops, and the majority of them had tattoos as intricate or more than Abbie's.

And speaking of Abbie, he couldn't spot her in the crowd of capoeiristas and spectators. Somehow, he'd expected something more like an actual performance—a stage for the players and seats for the spectators. But near as he could tell, it was just one big mass of people, milling about with no particular purpose or urgency. It made him uncomfortable. He was used to the rigid rules of a courtroom.

"Hey, Narc! You made it!" a male voice called out from behind him just as a large, strong hand smacked him in the back, sending him forward a few steps.

He turned to see the Brazilian man from the pool game. "Oh, hey," he managed to say after he recovered his breath. "Luiz, right?"

The man laughed. "Not today. Today it is Pintado. Only Pintado. You are looking for Boto, yes?"

"Boto, yes," Brunelle confirmed. "Is she around?"

"I'm sure she is," Pintado responded with a broad grin. "Perhaps she is in the Very Important Person area."

"Oh right," Brunelle responded. "Do I need like a badge or something?"

Pintado laughed, a big jolly head-tossing laugh. "No, no, my friend. There is no Very Important Person area. Everyone here is very important. Look around," he threw his arms wide. "Everyone here is here because they are welcome. There are no tickets and there are no Very Important Person passes."

"But, Abbie said…" Brunelle started.

"Boto tricked you," Pintado laughed again. "But do not be angry. She didn't care about the drinks. She cared about you."

Brunelle wasn't sure what to think. But he didn't get the time to figure it out. Pintado spotted Abbie.

"Boto!" he shouted over the crowd. "Boto! Your very important guest is here!"

Pintado gave him another hard slap on the shoulder and stepped away as Abbie made her way through the crowd to Brunelle.

"Hey, you made it!" she greeted him with a hug.

"Uh, yeah," Brunelle replied shakily. "So, there's no VIP pass, huh?"

Abbie smiled and looked after where Pintado had disappeared into the mass of people. "He ratted me out, huh? What do they say, snitches are bitches?"

Brunelle nodded. "Yeah. There's one about snitches ending up in ditches too. I prefer the term 'cooperating witness.'"

Abbie laughed. "You can take the narc out of the courtroom…, huh?"

"So, no VIP pass?" Brunelle repeated. "No tickets at all? You lied to me?"

Abbie tilted her head at him, dropping her thick blonde curls onto one shoulder. "Are you mad? You shouldn't be mad."

He wasn't, of course. "What should I be?"

Abbie smiled at him. "Flattered, of course." She grabbed his hand. "Now, come on. It's about to start. I can at least get you a VIP seat at the front."

'The front' meant a seat on the concrete floor where the crowd parted to create a large empty circle for the performers. Like theater-in-the-round, but more mosh pit than stage. Brunelle took his assigned spot and Abbie slipped away to where Pintado, Aguaviva, and the other capoeiristas stood waiting while their professor took the stage—or circle—to welcome everyone, including his own teacher all the way from Brazil.

"Hello, I am Professor Falcão," the man said in thickly accented English. He was on the short side, but with thick arms and broad shoulders. "Thank you all for coming to our batizado!"

The assembled crowd applauded and hollered, acknowledging their own awesomeness in having simply shown up.

"Before we begin, I would like to introduce to you my *graduados* and formados," Professor Falcão continued. "And then our very special guests from *Brasil*."

Falcão then announced each of his local senior students, each of whom came out to the circle and performed some moves that involved a kick, a flip, or a headstand, or some combination of those. When he announced Abbie—"Boto!"—she entered the circle at a sprint, did a flip, landed on her feet, then threw a roundhouse kick that came within inches of Professor Falcão's face. He didn't even flinch, confident in his student's ability not to break his nose. The crowds applauded, Brunelle as loudly as any of them.

The introductions continued until Boto, Pintado, Aguaviva, and the rest were standing behind their Brazilian sensei. Then it was time for the guest of honor.

"And now," Professor Falcão seemed genuinely moved to announce, "all the way from Rio de Janeiro, my mestre, and the leader of our studio, Mestre Águia!"

The crowd erupted into more cheers as Mestre Águia entered the circle. But no jumping or kicking for him. Just a slow, stately walk to embrace Professor Falcão in a bear hug. After several seconds, he turned and addressed the crowd—in Portuguese. Luckily for interlopers like Brunelle, Professor Falcão translated.

It was the usual stuff about thanking everyone for coming, how proud he was of his students and their students—the school-aged children waiting in the wings, also dressed in white pants and T-shirts with the smaller version of those silhouetted capoeiristas from the mural. Brunelle mostly kept his eyes on Abbie and let the foreign sounds roll over his ears, even as his knees started to wonder how long they were going to be twisted up on a cement floor.

Quite a while, as it turned out. The batizado was part skills showcase, part graduation ceremony. Each of those kids lined up against the wall was receiving a new belt—or cord, as they called it—to signify a move forward and up in their capoeira education. A lot of the adults were also moving up to new levels, and every one of them preceded the receipt of their cord with a display of the skills they had mastered in order to progress. All without bathroom breaks.

It was quite the show. The youngest capoeiristas, their parents making up at least half the crowd, mostly swayed to the Brazilian music played throughout the ceremony, with a few kicks and maybe a cartwheel. As the performers got older, the performances got more complex, and faster. By the time Abbie entered the circle, she and her compatriots were full-on sparring, their kicks narrowly missing one another's faces. But it was when Professor Falcão and Mestre Águia entered the circle that the crowd really got to see capoeira at its highest form. Flips, turns, cartwheels, handstands— all accompanied by lightning fast kicks, any one of which could have incapacitated the other man. It was an adrenaline-fueled blur of martial arts expertise. Brunelle didn't fully understand what was happening, but he was utterly and completely impressed nonetheless.

When, hours later, the batizado finally ended, Brunelle sought out Abbie—Boto—in the crowd.

"That was absolutely amazing," he enthused. "Just...wow!"

"Thanks." Abbie smiled as she took another drink from her water bottle. Her hair had lost a lot of its curl and was stuck to her neck with sweat, but somehow Brunelle found that even more attractive, or at least equally attractive, but in a different way. "Thanks. I'm glad you liked it."

"Thanks for inviting me," Brunelle said.

Abbie laughed. "I think you invited yourself. But I'm glad you came." She turned and looked around the garage-turned-studio. "What do you think of our studio? Pretty impressive, huh?"

"It used to be a garage, right?" Brunelle confirmed.

"Oh, yeah, definitely," Abbie confirmed with a grin. "This is a blast, but it's not exactly lucrative teaching lessons to a handful of kids. We needed the cheapest rent we could find, and this was it. You should have seen it before we cleaned it up. But hey," she gestured toward her sweaty body, "we're not afraid of a little hard work."

Brunelle tried not to be too obvious in admiring her hard work body. He nodded toward the painting on the wall behind her. "The mural is a nice touch. It really brightens the place up."

"Why, thank you," Abbie replied. "I did that myself."

Brunelle's eyebrows shot up. "You painted that?"

"I did," Abbie answered proudly. "I mean I got a little help filling in the figures once I'd gotten the outlines in far enough that they couldn't screw it up. But yeah, that's all me."

"Wow," Brunelle said for what seemed like the hundredth time since he'd arrived. "I had no idea you were an artist too."

"Too?" Abbie grinned. "You barely know anything about me to begin with."

Brunelle shrugged and thought for a moment. "I'd like to know more."

Abbie nodded. "I'd like that too." Then her face lit up. "Hey, I've got an art show coming up, actually. Nothing too big. Just a few of my paintings, along with some other local artists, but it's at an actual gallery. You should come."

"Absolutely," Brunelle was quick to agree. He pulled out his phone to check his calendar. "When is it?"

Abbie gave him the date and he entered it into his phone. "Oh, crap."

"What is it?" Abbie asked.

"Uh, I have a… conflict that night," Brunelle told her. Or rather, he half-told her.

"A conflict?" Abbie raised an eyebrow.

"Yeah, a conflict," Brunelle repeated.

When he didn't elucidate, Abbie frowned and nodded to herself. "Okay, well, never mind then. Obviously, a conflict is more important than some silly art show. At least you got to see my mural. Thanks for coming."

She turned to walk away. Brunelle reached out and grabbed her arm. "Wait. It's a work thing. Well, work-related."

Abbie didn't pull her arm away, but she just shrugged. "Sure. Work. I get it."

Brunelle sighed. He finally let go of her arm. "No, it's—Well, it's kind of embarrassing. But I don't want you to think I don't want to see your art."

"You care what I think?" Abbie asked.

Brunelle nodded.

"Then tell me the truth," she said. "I can't think the right thing if I don't know the truth."

Brunelle nodded again and took a deep breath. "I have to attend a sensitivity training class that night. Ordered by my Human Resources Department."

Abbie took a beat, then burst out laughing. "Sensitivity training? Really? Why? What happened?"

"I made a stupid joke to the wrong person," Brunelle explained. "This is my punishment. But I can't miss it. I could get fired if I don't go."

Abbie laughed some more. "That is awesome. A narc prosecutor who gets in trouble for breaking the rules. Perfect."

Brunelle forced a smile. "Glad you're entertained. I don't think the training will be quite so entertaining."

Abbie thought for a moment. "When is it? The training, what time does it start?"

Brunelle checked his phone again. "Uh, six o'clock. It runs two hours. God, I hope there's a break."

"So, you'll be done at eight?"

Brunelle shrugged. "Should be. Crap like this can run long, but once eight o'clock hits, I'm done. Time off for good behavior."

"Sounds like a time out for bad behavior," Abbie observed. "But no worries. The show runs from seven until nine. Come after your class. You'll be all sensitive and ready to be moved by my art."

"I'm not much of an art critic," Brunelle admitted.

"But you're a lawyer, right?" Abbie prompted.

When Brunelle nodded, Abbie grinned and winked at him. "Then you know how to lie to me."

CHAPTER 23

There were three types of lies. Lies, damn lies, and any time a lawyer opened his mouth. Well, at least if that lawyer was William Harrison Welles. And especially if there was a microphone in front of that mouth.

Brunelle arrived at the courthouse early the next morning. Early enough, he'd hoped, to avoid running into Welles at the metal detectors. But not early enough, apparently.

Welles was set up on the sidewalk outside the lesser used Fourth Avenue entrance. The main entrance on Third Avenue had too many homeless people milling about. He had his back to the building and was surrounded by a semi-circle of reporters and cameramen. There were only a half dozen total, but then again Seattle only had the usual four TV networks, so it was a good turnout for a local story, Brunelle supposed. It was likely to make a 90-second spot on the evening's news, unless a kitten got stuck in a tree or something.

Brunelle could see the press conference before he could hear it—kind of like lightning—but when he got close enough he was able to make out what Welles was saying.

"...a travesty..."

Of course, Brunelle thought sarcastically. *Totally inappropriate to hold someone accountable for killing another person.*

"...a true injustice..."

Right. Justice is for suckers.

"...and one borne not of sympathy for the victim..."

Well, jurors are instructed to let neither sympathy nor prejudice influence their verdict.

"...but of America's national shame. Racism."

"What?!" Brunelle blurted out just as he was almost past the show and safely inside the courthouse.

"Ah, my worthy opponent." Welles gestured toward Brunelle, a broad grin on his face.

Brunelle wondered if he'd actually timed that set of comments to provoke a reaction from him before he could get past the cameras. But Brunelle knew that was a silly question. Of course he had.

"This is Mr. David Brunelle," Welles informed the reporters, "the prosecutor who is midwifing this miscarriage of justice. Mr. Brunelle, would you like to address why you are prosecuting an innocent Asian man for the lawful use of force against a Caucasian aggressor?"

Brunelle grimaced. It was a 'When did you stop beating your wife?' question. If he simply said, 'No,' then technically he was saying, 'No, I don't want to address why I'm prosecuting an innocent Asian man for the lawful use of force against a Caucasian aggressor.' But if he said anything more he risked running afoul of the ethical rules on prosecutors regarding comments to the media. All Washington lawyers were governed by Rule of Professional Conduct 3.6 which prohibited making any statement that has 'a substantial likelihood of materially prejudicing an adjudicative proceeding'—whatever that meant. But prosecutors had their own additional rule, RPC 3.8, which prohibited a lot more, including 'extrajudicial comments that have a substantial likelihood of heightening public condemnation of the accused.' Just saying someone was guilty of a crime could probably meet that standard, if not worded very carefully. The safest thing for a prosecutor to say to the media was nothing. So Brunelle declined to answer the question for the cameras and addressed Welles directly instead.

"I thought we were here for a motion regarding expert testimony," he said. Definitely not sound-bitey enough to make a newscast.

But Welles wasn't deterred that easily.

"Ah, yes!" he bellowed. "An effort to deny my minority client his Constitutional right to confront his accusers. Tell me, Mr. Brunelle, do you believe no minorities should receive the protections enshrined in our Constitution, or just Asian-Americans? Maybe African-Americas, too? Probably African-Americans too, right?"

Brunelle thought for a moment, then turned away to walk into the courthouse.

"I will see you in court, sir!" Welles called out after him.

It took everything Brunelle had not to flip him off over his shoulder. That, caught on camera, would probably count as an 'extrajudicial statement' the Bar Association would frown upon.

* * *

They were in front of Judge Tillerson again, just like they would be for the trial. Same judge, same courtroom. Same bailiff and court reporter. Same defendant, of course, already seated at the defendant's table. One of the corrections officers was the same, but the other was new. And of course, same co-counsel, also already seated, but at the prosecutor's table.

"Morning, Gregory," Brunelle greeted him as his took his seat next to the young prosecutor.

"Morning, uh, Dave," Meckle returned. He looked nervously around the courtroom. "I don't see Mr. Welles yet."

"No, he's outside," Brunelle explained. "Multi-tasking."

Meckle shook his head slightly. "I don't understand."

"He's both poisoning the jury pool," Brunelle explained, "and marketing for his next case. Every case is an opportunity to advertise for his next case."

"Ah," Meckle replied in a way that showed he still didn't really understand what Brunelle was talking about.

"So," Brunelle changed the subject, a little anyway. "You ready to argue this motion?"

"Me?" Meckle squeaked. But then he smiled. "Oh, ha ha. Good one, Dave."

"No, I'm serious," Brunelle assured him. You wrote the brief, you argue the motion."

Meckle paused before responding. "Well, yeah. But, no. No, I'm not ready to argue this. I mean, I just assumed you were arguing it, so I didn't really prepare, you know?"

Brunelle nodded. "Ok. Sure. That makes sense."

Meckle sighed in relief. "So, you'll argue it?"

"Oh, no," Brunelle answered. "You're still arguing it. I was just acknowledging that you aren't ready, that's all."

Meckle looked first shocked, then ready to protest, but Welles entered the courtroom then, quite loudly, and saved Brunelle from further entreaties from his co-counsel.

"You can set up back here," Welles was informing the cameramen who had followed him into the courtroom. "Maybe put your microphones on my table down front."

The bailiff popped up and hurried toward the back of the courtroom. "No, no, no. The judge only allows one camera. You'll have to share the footage. And the microphone will go on the lower bench, in front of the court reporter. We have a procedure for this sort of thing."

Welles smiled and left the media to the care of the bailiff. He strutted down to the defense table and slapped his client heartily in the back. "Ready, Jeremy?"

Nguyen nodded. "Sure."

"They treating you okay?" Welles followed up as he set his briefcase down and began extracting his materials for the hearing.

Another nod. "Sure. Yeah."

"Good, good," Welles said. Then he pointed at Brunelle and Meckle. "What about these two, huh?"

Brunelle was surprised by the question. Those same rules that prevented him from talking to the media made it absolutely clear he could never, ever talk to a represented defendant.

"Uh, I don't know," Nguyen answered. "I mean, they're trying to put me in prison, right? So..."

"That they are, that they are," Welles confirmed. "Good. You're paying attention."

"It's hard not to pay attention to you, Welles," Brunelle sniped.

But Welles just grinned broadly. "I know."

Judge Tillerson emerged from his chambers at that moment. The bailiff, who was still in the back arguing with the media, called out a belated, "All rise!" and hurried back to the front of the courtroom.

"Are the parties ready?" Tillerson asked after he'd taken his seat above them.

"Yes, Your Honor," Brunelle stood to answer.

Welles, who hadn't had the chance to sit down, offered a confident, "Absolutely, Your Honor. Ready and eager."

Tillerson acknowledged the response with a grunt. "That's just great. Okay, Mr. Welles, this is your motion. I'll hear first from you."

"Thank you, Your Honor." Welles stepped away from the defense table and positioned himself awkwardly to one side, so he could both address the Court, and be filmed from the back without blocking the frame of the classic courtroom shot. "Allow me to begin by declaring that it pained me to have to bring this motion, Your Honor. I take no pleasure in accusing a career prosecutor," he gestured at Brunelle, "of unethical and immoral, if not perhaps also illegal, conduct. But I give no quarter when defending the Constitutional rights of my clients."

Oh, brother, Brunelle thought. He decided to just take notes, to discourage himself from looking at Welles as he attacked him. The classic defense technique. Distract from the accusations against the defendant by accusing the police and prosecutors of allegedly worse misconduct. There was a statute against murder, but Brunelle had, apparently, violated the Constitution. Insert gasp here.

"I see the cameras, Mr. Welles," Judge Tillerson interrupted. "But there's no need to cast personal aspersions."

"Not personal aspersions," Welles responded with a flourish of his hand. "Professional aspersions. I know Mr. Brunelle. Which is to say, I am professionally acquainted with him. I have no reason to believe he holds any personal animosity, outside of his job, against my client or any other minority. But here and now, as a prosecutor, as a quasi-judicial officer charged, not with obtaining a conviction at any cost, but with protecting the rights of the accused as much as seeking to vindicate those of the alleged victim, he nevertheless most likely never gives a second thought to how his individual actions on individual cases conspire to convict innocent men, and doom them to live in cages for the rest of their lives."

Brunelle leaned over to Meckle. "It's not life," he whispered. "He's looking at twenty-five years, thirty max."

"So," Welles continued, "it is with no joy that I accuse Mr. Brunelle of attempting to deny my client of that most basic of Constitutional rights, the core of all the others and the bedrock of the Anglo-American criminal judicial system. Of course, I speak of the right of an accused to confront the witnesses against him. To subject those witnesses to the vigorous cross-examination from which the truth might be divined by the finder of fact."

Welles glanced back at the cameras to make sure they were still rolling, then continued.

"Our entire system of criminal justice—the greatest system ever developed—is based on the infinitely simple, yet infinitely important principle that the jury," he pointed to the empty jury box, "must decide the case based, not on what happened out there," a gesture toward the door to the hallway, "but rather on what happened in here," a final gesture, pointing at the floor in the center of the courtroom. "The State must prove, in here, and beyond a reasonable doubt, that my client committed each and every element of the crime charged. And yet, they would endeavor to do so based on statements made outside this courtroom. Statements made by the medical examiner who conducted the autopsy, memorialized in her pathology report, but statements which were never subjected to the crucible of truth, cross-examination by an advocate, not for the State or the police or the deceased, but an advocate for the one accused of the murder. The one who, if convicted, will spend the rest his life in the aforementioned cage."

"I wish he'd stop saying 'cage'," Meckle whispered to Brunelle. "That sounds terrible. It's called a cell."

Brunelle shrugged. "Which is a cage," he understood.

"And Your Honor," Welles continued with another flourish of his hand, pointing at the sky, "this principle is so fundamental, so revered, so sacred, that it was enshrined in our very Constitution. In the Bill of Rights no less, alongside such paragons of liberty as freedom of speech and the separation of church and state.

"But here, now, with this man," Welles took a moment to extend a sympathetic hand toward his belly-chained client, "the State, through Mr. Brunelle, would deprive me the opportunity to cross-examine the person he himself represented to the Court at the last hearing is the single most important witness in this entire case. Dr. Marianne Delacourt, the Assistant Medical Examiner who conducted the autopsy upon which the State intends to build its house of cards of a case.

"Your Honor will recall, it was this autopsy which Mr. Brunelle endorsed as the purported basis for all of the conclusions the State will ask the jury to draw to support its tenuous, fanciful, I dare say delusional theory that my client did anything that fateful night other than exercise his right to use lawful force in defending himself against imminent harm from an armed assailant."

Welles took a moment, drawing a deep breath and steepling his fingers in front of his chest.

"The autopsy, conducted by Dr. Delacourt, purportedly shows that the alleged victim never fired his own firearm. The autopsy, conducted by Dr. Delacourt, purportedly shows that my client was several feet away when he fired his own weapon. The autopsy, conducted by Dr. Delacourt, purportedly shows that the precision of the shot to the alleged victim's forehead evinces premeditation.

"And yet!" Welles shouted the phrase, then repeated it. "And yet, the State intends *not* to call Dr. Delacourt as a witness against my client. Instead, they propose to call a different pathologist. One who did not conduct the autopsy. One who was not present for the autopsy. One who can therefore do no more than read Dr. Delacourt's autopsy report. And one, therefore, who is impervious to cross-examination, being able, honestly, to answer, 'I don't know,' to any question I put to him in order to challenge Dr. Delacourt's alleged findings or the inferences therefrom upon which the State would base its otherwise baseless case."

Welles raised a hand to his chin and raised his gaze thoughtfully. "I believe it was young Abraham Lincoln, already building his well-earned reputation as a skillful and inventive trial attorney, who said, 'It is no overstatement to say that the institution of cross-examination is the cornerstone upon which the foundation of our nation of laws is built.'"

Brunelle rolled his eyes. "Lincoln never said that," he whispered to Meckle.

"Are you a Lincoln expert?" he asked.

"No, I'm a Welles expert," Brunelle answered. "But don't worry. That means I can tell he's almost done. He usually ends with a powerful quote, even if he has to make it up."

"Finally, Your Honor," Welles continued.

"See?" Brunelle whispered. "Told ya."

"As much as it pains me to raise this additional issue," Welles said, "this added wrinkle, if you will, to the prosecutor's already indefensible effort to deprive my client of his sacrosanct Constitutional rights, but I would be remiss in my duties to my client, and indeed my duties to this Court and our system of justice as a whole, if I were to notice it and then fail to bring it into the cleansing light of day."

"What is he talking about?" Meckle whispered to Brunelle.

But Brunelle didn't answer. He knew what was coming, and in front of the camera too.

"But one cannot simply overlook the fact," Welles proceeded, "that the decedent in this case, although armed, was a person of the Caucasian persuasion. And my client, as you can see, is not. I wonder, would the State have been so quick to dismiss my client's timely and heartfelt explanation of self-defense were the roles reversed? Were it a white man who had shot a person of color who'd had a loaded firearm in his brown, or black, or tan hand?"

"Okay. That's enough." Brunelle stood up. "I object."

Tillerson nodded. "I agree that Mr. Welles's argument may seem personally offensive, but he is advocating on behalf of his client. What is the legal basis for your objection?"

Brunelle thought for a moment. "It wasn't in his brief."

The judge raised an eyebrow. "Lack of notice? Your objection is lack of notice?"

"Sure," Brunelle agreed.

Tillerson raised that eyebrow a bit higher. "Do you really want to set this part of his argument over for a special hearing on whether you're a racist?"

Brunelle thought for a moment. He didn't look back at the reporters and their camera, but he was aware of them. And he knew they'd definitely be back for that type of a hearing. And an encore performance by William Harrison Welles.

"I suppose not," Brunelle agreed. Besides he'd accomplished his real goal of interrupting Welles's flow. "I withdraw the objection."

"I thought so," Judge Tillerson said not entirely under his breath. "Back to you, Mr. Welles. Do you have anything you want to add to your argument that the prosecutor is a racist conspiring to deprive your client of his Constitutional rights?"

Welles thought for a moment. "No, Your Honor," he answered. "Except to say—"

"So, yes," Tillerson corrected him.

Welles smiled. "Indeed, Your Honor. Except to say that Your Honor should focus, not on the subjective intent of Mr. Brunelle, or any other prosecutor for that matter, but rather on the objective results inflicted upon my client. He has a right to confront and cross-examine the witnesses against him. We implore Your Honor to safeguard that right and hold the State to basic standards of fairness and decency in their misguided attempts to imprison an innocent man. Thank you."

With that, Welles offered a slight bow to Judge Tillerson, and another, less perceptible one to the camera in the back, before taking his seat next to his client, who seemed quite pleased with his lawyer's performance.

Well, they ain't seen nothing yet, Brunelle thought sardonically.

Judge Tillerson turned to the prosecution table. "Response, Mr. Brunelle?" he prompted.

Brunelle stood up to address the judge, but it was that awkward, still half squatting stand that indicated he intended to sit right back down again. "Actually, Your Honor, Mr. Meckle will be delivering the response on behalf of the State."

Tillerson took a moment. "Really?"

"Yeah," Meckle whispered at Brunelle. "Really?"

"Really," Brunelle confirmed, that time without standing.

"Even," the judge inquired, "after Mr. Welles called you an unethical racist?"

"Especially," Brunelle answered, "after he called me an unethical racist."

Tillerson took another moment, then sighed. "Very well. Mr. Meckle, is it?"

"Uh, yes, Your Honor," Meckle confirmed as he stood up. He took a few seconds to fumble with his copy of his brief and his notepad full of notes from Welles's argument, before setting them both aside again and looking up at the judge. He was still behind the prosecution table. "Okay. Um, thank you, Your Honor. May it please the Court, counsel, uh, the media, I guess. I am Gregory Meckle, Assistant District Attorney, on behalf of the State of Washington."

Judge Tillerson sighed again and looked back to Brunelle. "Really?" he repeated.

Brunelle nodded. "Really."

The judge nodded as well, and leaned back in his chair. "Okay. Go on, Mr. Meckle. Get to your argument, please."

"Uh, yes, Your Honor," Meckle responded. "Thank you, Your Honor. Uh, so… The State believes… That is… Uh, has Your Honor had a chance to read my brief?"

Brunelle lowered his face into his hand.

"Did I read your brief?" Judge Tillerson clarified.

"Yes, Your Honor," Meckle affirmed.

"You mean, did I do my job?" Tillerson asked. "Did I prepare for this very important hearing on a first-degree murder case?"

"Uh, I mean, well, yes," Meckle answered.

"Yes," Tillerson practically growled. "I read your brief, counsel."

"Ah, yes, well, that's good. Thank you, Your Honor." Meckle took a moment to gather his thoughts and Brunelle raised his head again. He didn't want to miss whatever show was about to take place.

"Well, as I point out in my brief," Meckle began, "the evidence rules and the relevant case law provide ample authority for the proposition that one expert can testify regarding the findings of another expert, so long as there is a comity of expertise. That is, so long as the testifying expert is an expert on the same subject matter as the non-testifying expert is an expert."

"I know what 'comity' means, counsel," Tillerson interjected.

"Yes, of course you do," Meckle apologized.

"But what about Mr. Welles's argument," the judge asked, "that calling Dr. Kleinbart instead of Dr. Delacourt deprives the defendant of his rights under the Confrontation Clause? Do the evidence rules and case law trump the Constitution?"

"Well, no, of course not," Meckle conceded. "But they were written, and decided, I'm sure, with the Constitution in mind."

But Judge Tillerson frowned. "I'm not so certain of that. Let me ask you what I feel is the real heart of the question here. No one is claiming that Dr. Kleinbart isn't qualified to give an expert opinion regarding an autopsy. The real question is, why are you calling him? Why aren't you just calling Dr. Delacourt? She did the autopsy. Isn't she the best person to testify about her own findings? I mean, wouldn't that be better for the State as well?"

"Uh..." Meckle hesitated. He looked to Brunelle. "I, uh, I'm not entirely sure, Your Honor."

Brunelle sighed, then stood up. "Dr. Delacourt has expressed a preference not to work directly with me, Your Honor."

Whatever Judge Tillerson might have been expecting, his expression showed it wasn't that. "Oh, really? And why is that?"

Brunelle shrugged. "Probably because I'm an unethical racist."

But Tillerson frowned. "That's not funny."

Brunelle shrugged again. "It's kind of funny."

"Is Dr. Delacourt otherwise available?" the judge asked. "Apart from her personal aversion to working with you?"

"As far as I know," Brunelle answered.

Tillerson thought for a moment, then looked to the calendar hanging on the wall. "Trial is scheduled to begin two weeks from today. Do you think you can work out whatever difference you have with the good doctor so she can be ready to testify by then?"

"Your Honor," Brunelle nodded, "if you order the State to call her and not Dr. Kleinbart, then I believe I can use that ruling to convince her to make herself available to testify at trial."

Judge Tillerson looked down at him. "You want to lose this motion?"

"What I want, Your Honor," Brunelle answered, "is to do my job, to the best of my abilities. That includes both putting on the best possible case while at the same time protecting the defendant's Constitutional rights."

"Is that why you had your co-counsel argue the motion?" Tillerson asked.

"Yeah, is it?" Meckle joined.

"No," Brunelle replied. "He argued it because he wrote the brief. He did the research. And he's right. The evidence rules and the case law do say it's okay in some circumstances, despite the Confrontation Clause."

"But it's not okay, is it?" Tillerson asked him.

Brunelle deflected. "It's not if you say it's not. And if you say it's not, then Dr. Delacourt will appear to testify in person against Mr. Nguyen."

"So, it's all on me?" the judge asked.

"Well, you are the judge," Brunelle pointed out. "But no. There's one thing I'll have to do before trial as well."

Judge Tillerson took a few moments to consider everything he'd just heard. It was customary to allow the moving party—Welles—a brief opportunity to respond to the State's argument, but it wasn't necessary if the judge was going to rule in Welles's favor. Which he was.

"All right, then," the judge announced, "the defense motion is granted. Dr. Kleinbart may not testify in lieu of Dr. Delacourt because doing so would violate the defendant's right to confront witnesses against him under both the Sixth Amendment to the United States Constitution and Article One, Section Twenty-Two, of the Washington State Constitution."

"Thank you, Your Honor," Welles stood to accept the ruling.

But Tillerson just grinned down at him from the bench. "Be careful what you wish for, Mr. Welles."

Then the judge turned to Brunelle. "If the good doctor still refuses to testify, I think you'll find it hard to prove a murder without evidence regarding the cause of death. I've done my part, Mr. Brunelle. I would advise you to do yours. Whatever it is."

"Understood," Brunelle answered. "I will."

CHAPTER 24

They say 90% of life is just showing up. But it was 100% of mandatory HR training following a complaint of sexual harassment, or sexual discrimination, or whatever it was exactly that he did. It was two hours of his life Brunelle knew he was never going to get back, but it was only hours of listening to someone lecture him—not days of further interviews, weeks of investigation, months of looking for another job, and years of wrongful termination litigation. A small price to pay.

The class was in a small room on the third floor of the King County Administration Building, which stood between the courthouse and the jail.

Apropos, Brunelle thought as he arrived.

There were seven other 'students'—all white men over 40. Brunelle was honest enough with himself to suppose that was probably the demographic most in need of whatever education he was about to receive. The instructors were a male/female team in their late 20s or early 30s, smiling a little too much as they greeted everyone entering the stuffy little room.

Chairs had been set up in four rows of four, all facing a whiteboard at the front. Brunelle took a seat in the middle of the front row and put on his best face. He needed to pass the class so he could put this all behind him, and get Dr. Delacourt in front of the jury. So, no jokes, despite the absolute certainty of at least one opportunity for a solid 'that's what she said.' And no other comments or interruptions. That would only slow things down. He would keep his mouth shut unless he was asked a question, and if asked a question, he would give what he knew the right answer was, regardless of whether it was true.

"Okay!" the woman teacher chimed as everyone else took their seats and she closed the classroom door. "It looks like everyone made it. I'm Mandy, and this is Jeff, and we're going to be your co-leaders on tonight's very important, sometimes difficult, but ultimately extremely rewarding journey."

"That's right, Mandy!" Jeff pealed back.

Brunelle forced a smile. It was going to be a long two hours. But he took inspiration from the name of his offense: sexual harassment. He decided he would split his evening in two, sex and harassment. In the first part, he would let himself be harassed by Mandy and Jeff. And in the second part, he could try to get…

"Abbie!" Brunelle called out as he entered the art gallery and saw her standing a few feet from the entrance, looking somehow both proud and nervous at the same time.

"Narc!" She called back. "You made it."

"Wouldn't miss it for the world," he assured her. "How's it going?"

The gallery wasn't exactly full, but it wasn't completely empty either. A few people more than the class he'd just left, counting Mandy and Jeff. Although some of those appeared to be other artists, judging by their similar expressions of pride/fear.

"Pretty well, I think." Abbie shrugged. "I mean, I haven't sold anything, but that's not really the point. I mean, it's sort of the point. I'd love to sell something. But really, it's just about getting your art up on the wall for people to see, you know?"

Brunelle didn't. But he said he did. Of course.

"Wanna see some of my stuff?" Abbie asked with a broad smile, the anxiety melting away to let the pride shine through.

Brunelle did want that. If nothing else, he was curious. Would it all be silhouettes of dancing, fighting capoeiristas? The answer, of course and most definitely, was no.

The gallery consisted of two large rooms, with a freestanding wall in the center right corner of each. Abbie had eight pieces up, each different from the last, in her assigned space in the back corner of the first room. Abbie led him to her exhibit space and started the art tour.

"All these are yours?" Brunelle asked, surprised. He was no artist, but he'd expected a series of similar paintings. Maybe not silhouetted athletes, but perhaps a series of watercolor landscapes, or impressionistic portraits. Some unifying style that let the viewer know they had sprung from the same artist. But no. "They're so... so different."

Abbie surveyed her artwork quickly and grinned. "Thanks."

The nearest piece was that watercolor landscape Brunelle had anticipated. Actually, he didn't know if it was watercolor, but it was definitely a landscape. A lonely field, a tree in the distance, gray clouds hanging low and heavy. Next on the wall was also on a canvas—or something like it—but involved much more than paint, with metal, glass, and ceramic protruding at him, forming a pattern he felt sure eluded him. Then something that looked like a kaleidoscope melted on a plank of wood. A sculpture of a winged woman alighted from a pedestal in the corner. The next wall started with another canvas, with an incredibly lifelike portrait of a young, dirty-faced girl. Another landscape, but this time an urban scene, somehow both desolate and hopeful. And at the end was something Brunelle couldn't even describe. It was like all of the other works put together on an enormous frame, canvas extending over some, but not all of the space inside.

"Wow," he exhaled once he'd taken in all of it. "I don't know what to say."

"Say what you're thinking," Abbie reassured. "I can take it, good or bad."

"No, that's just it," Brunelle tried to explain. "I don't know what to say. I don't know enough about art to know what to say about this. I'm awestruck. Each one is so powerful. But I bet there's so much more I don't understand. I didn't go to art school. I don't know how you did all this. I know I like it. I just wish I could explain why."

Abbie laughed a little and shook her head. "It's art, Dave. You don't have to justify how it makes you feel. That's kind of the point, actually."

Brunelle nodded, almost absently, at her words, then pointed at the final piece, the one with the flat paint and raised items and missing canvas. "Tell me about this one."

Abbie looked at it for a moment. "What do you want to know?"

Brunelle thought for a moment. "Why is there extra stuff on it? The metal and wood sticking out. Why not just paint?"

"It's called mixed media," Abbie explained. "It lets me actually explore all three dimensions, rather than create the illusion of three dimensions with only two."

She gestured toward the urchin portrait, but Brunelle couldn't take his eyes off the artwork in front of him.

"What about the holes?" He pointed at the gaps in the canvas, barely able to resist the urge to stick a finger into the void beyond. "What do those mean?"

"Anything you want," Abbie answered.

But Brunelle wasn't having it. "No, come on. Really. Why the empty space? Why not just leave the canvas blank in those spots?"

Abbie thought for a moment. "I guess I'm not sure, really. I wanted to have nothing, absolutely nothing. Empty canvas would have been, well, empty, but it still would have been there. But sometimes, I don't know, you want nothing. Absolutely nothing. A blank asks to be filled in, but nothing demands you to accept it as it is."

Brunelle nodded. "Yeah. I've heard something like that before."

"Really?" Abbie asked. "From another artist you were trying to date?"

Brunelle was still mesmerized by the artwork, so he missed Abbie's joke. "No," he said, "a cop."

"You were trying to date a cop?"

"What?" Brunelle shook his head. "No. I mean, not that cop anyway.

Det. Chen. Larry."

Abbie laughed. "What did Detective Larry say?"

"He said I should embrace the holes in my case, and stop trying to fill them with something that I might not like after all."

Abbie looked at her artwork again and shrugged. "Not sure that's exactly what I was trying to say here, but I'm glad it spoke to you anyway."

Brunelle nodded for several moments, still staring at Abbie's art, but his mind never really that far from his own work. "I guess it's time to let Joan Inha go."

"If you say so." Abbie shrugged. Then his eyebrows drew together. "Wait. Did you say 'Joan Inha'?" She exaggerated the syllables in the name.

Brunelle nodded. "Yeah. That's who I was looking for when I met you. She's a witness on my latest case. Or maybe a witness. Her name was on a scrap of paper the victim had in his pocket."

"Joan Inha?" Abbie repeated. Then she spelled it, "J-O-A-N-I-N-H-A?"

"Yeah," Brunelle confirmed. "Common spelling, or whatever."

Abbie began chuckling, then, seeing Brunelle's puzzled expression, broke out into a full belly laugh. "It's not 'Joan Inha', you dope. It's *joaninha*," pronouncing it 'zhoh-ah-nee-nya.' "It's Portuguese for 'ladybug.' And it's the capoeira name of Mestre Águia's wife."

CHAPTER 25

"Come on, Larry. Pick up. Pick up." Brunelle was out on the sidewalk and dialing Chen's number faster than Abbie could say, "Where are you going?" Which is exactly what she did say when Brunelle bolted out of the art gallery to call his lead detective.

He half expected her to follow him outside. She didn't. Which was fine by him. He was done with the art show. He had work to do.

"Hello?" Chen finally picked up.

"Larry! It's Dave. I figured it out. I know who Joan Inha is."

"Are you fucking kidding me?" Chen barked over the phone. "You're calling me about that again?"

"Joan Inha isn't Joan Inha." Brunelle ignored Chen's complaint. "Joan Inha is Zho-uh-nin-er-something. Shit. It's a word, not a name. Well, it's a name too, but in Portuguese. Well, no, in Portuguese it's a word. It means ladybug. But it's also somebody's name. Sort of."

There was a long pause. Finally, Chen asked, "Are you drunk?"

"I've never been more sober!" Brunelle declared. "I mean, I don't know. I guess sober is sober. You can't really be extra sober, really. But yeah, I'm sober. And I know who Joaninha is."

There was a long pause as Chen took in the information. Finally, he sighed. "Do you know how late it is? And how early I have to get to work in the morning?"

"It's not that late," Brunelle returned. "And anyway, isn't this what detectives do? Stay up late, cracking cases, cleaning up the streets, protecting and serving and stuff?"

"Ugh." Another sigh. "Do you have a real name? Not a Portuguese nickname? And how the hell do you know Portuguese all of a sudden?"

"I don't," Brunelle explained, "but Abbie does."

"Abbie?" Chen repeated. "Ah. Okay. No, of course. This all makes sense now. Abbie is your latest girlfriend?"

"No," Brunelle said. "Not exactly. Not yet. Maybe not at all. I don't know. But she knows Joaninha and she knows where we can find her. I think."

"You think?"

"Uh, yeah," Brunelle hesitated. "I guess I didn't actually ask her that. Um, hold on."

"Ask for a real name too," Chen suggested.

"Right," Brunelle acknowledged.

He walked back to the very front of the gallery and peered inside. Abbie was standing about halfway between the entrance and her exhibit, her eyes on the door. Brunelle tapped on the glass to get her attention.

She turned to look at him and offered a 'what the hell?' gesture: eyes wide, a shake of the head, palms thrown to the side. He responded with a 'come outside' gesture: a roll of the wrist and pointing toward the door. She replied with an exasperated shrug and eyes to the ceiling. But then she stormed out to the sidewalk.

"What are you doing?" she demanded. "I invited you to my showing so you could see my art, not so you could get one of my friends in trouble."

"No one's going to get in trouble," Brunelle promised. "Except Jeremy Nguyen. But not Joaninha. I just need you to tell me her real name and where I can find her." She glanced at the phone in his hand, the call still open. "I've got the lead detective on the line right now. We can go talk to her tonight. Straighten this all out."

"Straighten what out?" Abbie questioned. "Maria didn't kill anyone. She just came here for the batizado."

"Okay, her first name is Maria," Brunelle seized on that information. "Great. What's her last name?"

Abbie cocked her head at him. "Really? That's all you care about? Tracking down my mestre's wife? What about my show? What about me? What about how this is going to impact my relationship with everyone at the studio? I can't narc out the mestre's wife."

"You're not narcking anyone out," Brunelle insisted. "She's a witness, not a suspect. I just need to know why the dead man had her name in his pocket. I need to know the motive for the murder."

"You don't even know the motive?" Abbie questioned.

"No, but I'm about to," Brunelle answered. "If you'll just tell me where I can find her."

CHAPTER 26

Maria Oliveira, a.k.a. Joaninha the ladybug, and her husband Carlos Oliveira, a.k.a. Mestre Águia the eagle, were staying at a small hotel in the International District, just a few blocks from the capoeira studio. Brunelle went straight there to wait for Chen while he ran Maria's real name for any information he might be able to find. It was a long shot they would find anything—Seattle P.D. didn't have access to Brazilian police or court records—but it was worth the look, just in case.

When Chen finally arrived, he had both papers in his hand and a partner at his side.

"Hey, Dave," Montero greeted him as they walked up to where he was standing at the entrance to the hotel. "Larry says we're here to get Portuguese lessons? How do you say 'wild goose chase'?"

Brunelle grimaced. "Ha. But really, this is the best lead we've had to figure out why Nguyen shot Peter Ostrander."

"Hm," Chen harrumphed. "We'll see. Honestly, this doesn't make a lot of sense. Why would a white guy who got shot by a Vietnamese guy in Chinatown have the Portuguese nickname of a Brazilian tourist in his pocket?"

"I know, right?" Brunelle agreed. "The jury is gonna want to know that. *I* want to know that."

But Chen shook his head. "Be careful what you wish for."

Brunelle cocked his own head, encouraging more explanation from his detective, but Chen just laughed to himself and grabbed the door. "C'mon. Let's get this over with. I promised Evie I'd be home before bed."

"You don't want to disappoint Mrs. Chen," Brunelle observed.

Chen smiled, but didn't laugh again. "No, I do not."

The interior of the hotel belied its meager origins. Looking past the tourism and shopping benefits of a Chinatown, there were less benign reasons why those districts existed. Immigrants from East Asia weren't allowed to live intermixed with the white settlers who'd established their society on top of the Native land they'd appropriated. It wasn't until 1966 that Washington State finally repealed the 'Alien Land Laws' that had originally been designed to prevent Asian immigrant laborers from not only owning land, but even renting it.

Those laborers, seeking a better life, but underpaid and overlooked, just needed a small room, big enough for a bed, with a communal bathroom at the end of the hall, and walking distance to the docks or the rail yard or the lumber mills where they might find work. The result was a tiny lobby, with no windows to the outside, overly decorated in reds and golds. A yellowed glass chandelier hung over the reception desk, a steep staircase rising to its right, a narrow hallway disappearing to its left. An older Asian man, his black hair frosted with white, stood up as the three of them entered. Chen did the talking, for more reasons than one.

"Hello," he started. "I'm Detective Larry Chen of the Seattle Police Department. We're hoping you can help us find someone we need to talk to."

Technically, in Washington anyway, the police needed a warrant to seize a hotel's guest book. Guests had a privacy interest in their residences, even temporary ones, and that interest was protected by Article I, Section 7, of the Washington State Constitution. But also technically, cops could always ask. Kind of like *Miranda*: 'You have the right to remain silent, but would you be willing to answer a few questions?' Most suspects agreed to talk, even when they knew they were guilty. So, if a hotel clerk was willing to tell law enforcement where a particular guest was, well, then that would be between the hotel and the guest—but the cops didn't have to ignore the information.

"Thank you, sir," Chen replied after the hotelier told him that Maria and Carlos Oliveira were staying in Room 312. "Is there an elevator?"

The man indicated the hallway, but Montero slapped her partner on the arm. "Let's take the stairs, old man. It's only two floors."

In the event, it was three. The 100-numbered rooms were on the first floor above the lobby, and so on. Old school. Or Old World, anyway. Whichever it was, Brunelle was out of breath by the time they reached what was, by traditional American standards anyway, the fourth floor.

The hallway was as narrow and windowless as the lobby, with room doors on either side, and close enough together to reveal the minimal interior dimensions of the rooms behind them. Room 312 was going to be on the left-hand side, with the other even numbers, and about halfway down the hallway. Again, Chen led the way. Again, Brunelle was happy to let him. He wanted to know how Joaninha knew Peter Ostrander, but he was content to listen to the answers to questions posed by the professional interrogators.

When they reached Room 312, Chen took a moment to assess it—nothing out of the ordinary—then knocked. Three sharp raps.

There was no immediate answer. Then, after that amount of time when it was time to knock a second time, Chen put a little more into it. He rapped his knuckles four times and added, "Mr. and Mrs. Oliveira?"

Again, there was no answer. Again, they waited the socially agreed amount of time before it was okay to knock a third time. Brunelle sighed and leaned against the opposite wall, realizing he hadn't accounted for the possibility that no one would be there when they went.

"Maybe they're out to dinner?" he suggested.

Montero turned to Brunelle and frowned. "It's a little late for dinner, but yeah, maybe."

Chen sighed and tried one more time. He switched to a pounding with the side of his fist, and a more formal announcement: "Mr. and Mrs. Oliveira. This is the police. Please open the door."

Brunelle hadn't thought about it at the time, but he'd taken a step and half to the right of the doorway when he'd leaned against the wall, to find a spot between the narrowly spaced doors. He also hadn't noticed it, but Montero had taken a half step toward him when she responded to his supposition about the Oliveiras' dinner plans. But Chen was standing directly in front of the door when the gunshots from inside tore through the old wooden door—and Chen's completely unarmored body.

"Shit!" Brunelle dove away from the door.

Montero dropped to the floor as well, right next to Chen, who was collapsed in a bleeding heap against the far wall.

She pulled out her handgun and her police-issued phone. "Officer down! Officer down!" she shouted into the phone. "Oh, God, Larry's down!"

CHAPTER 27

Montero took up a defensive position a few feet to one side of the bullet-shattered door to Room 312. She didn't dare move Chen, lest she make whatever injuries he'd suffered even worse.

"Officer down," she repeated into her phone, even as she kept her eyes, and her pistol, trained on the Oliveiras' hotel room. "Active shooter situation. Need priority backup and medical aid immediately. Hotel Jackson. Room 312."

Then she turned her head slightly to Brunelle, without taking her eyes off the hotel room door. "Get out of here."

Brunelle hesitated. Partly because he didn't want to abandon his friend. Partly because Montero, Chen, and whoever was shooting out of Room 312 were all between him and the stairs.

"I can stay," he offered weakly.

"Now," Montero ordered. "You're a liability. Don't make me arrest you for obstruction. Go."

Brunelle nodded. A lawyer with no gun. There was nothing he could possibly do, except maybe help direct the backup officers to the room when they arrived. He looked again at his friend, crumpled in a bloody pile just a few feet away. Chen's eyes were closed, but his chest was still rising, albeit with labored breaths.

"Okay," Brunelle agreed. The elevator was probably at the other end of the hallway. He got up carefully, then ran to the end of the hallway and pressed the down button repeatedly until the elevator finally made its way up from the lobby.

The next few hours were a blur. Brunelle made it safely downstairs and out onto the front sidewalk. Backup arrived seconds later. He was removed to a safe distance as S.W.A.T. took over the building. He didn't know exactly what was going on inside, but he knew the police had two goals: extract Chen and get him to the hospital, and neutralize the shooter or shooters, whether by arrest or deadly force. No one was going to question them killing an attempted cop killer.

Brunelle watched and waited until finally a gurney emerged from the hotel and was loaded hastily into a waiting ambulance. That had to be Chen. And he had to be going to Harborview, the top emergency trauma hospital in the entire Pacific Northwest. It was also the closest. You could see it from the International District, looking down from its perch on First Hill, just east of downtown. That was where Chen was going, so that's where Brunelle was going too.

He had to walk a few blocks before he flagged down a taxi. By the time he got to the hospital, Chen was already in surgery. The hospital would never tell him whether or where a particular patient was—they weren't the night guy at some hotel in Chinatown—but Brunelle knew where the emergency surgery center was, and he knew Evie Chen when he saw her in the waiting room, flanked by their teenage kids, all of them sick with worry and disbelief.

"Oh, Dave!" she called out when she saw him. She hugged him, her tears damp against his neck. "What happened?"

"I—I don't know," he admitted. "But I'll find out. I promise."

CHAPTER 28

In the event, it wasn't Brunelle who found out what happened; it was the police, including but limited to Montero. Brunelle didn't need to be there for the interrogation of someone who shot a cop. He just needed to know the results, not the methods that might jeopardize the admissibility of those results in court. There wasn't an official 'officer down' exception to the rules cops were supposed to follow. But there weren't a lot of judges who would penalize it either if, in the heat of that particular moment, some of the standard protocols were shortcut.

They'd been able to take Maria Oliveira alive. That in itself was amazing, since there probably wasn't a cop in that hotel who wanted her alive. Or at least, there wasn't one who would shed a tear if she'd given them any excuse at all to shoot her. But when they finally entered the hotel room, they'd found her in the middle of the room, kneeling on the floor, hands on her head, and her gun out of reach, several feet in front of her. Her English, and her instincts, were good enough to immediately say, "I give up."

Still, the handcuffing was probably rougher than it needed to be. Same with being put in the back of the patrol car for the trip to the downtown station. She was probably offered a lawyer at some point—the forms certainly made it look that way—but they didn't wait for a Portuguese interpreter. Third parties tended to make people behave better, and no one sitting opposite Joaninha in that interrogation room was really feeling like being on best behavior.

Montero led the interrogation, with two other detectives in the room. They didn't record it—another red flag, but not one that rendered her statements inadmissible at any future court proceeding. Like her trial for shooting Chen. Attempted Murder One.

At least, Brunelle hoped it would stay 'attempted.' Chen was still in a medically induced coma when Montero stopped by his office the next afternoon to drop off her report of the interrogation.

"What did she say?" he asked even as he took the report from her.

"She said she panicked," Montero said as she sat down across from Brunelle. "The police in Brazil aren't as hung up on due process as we are, I guess. Running drugs can land you in prison for the rest of your life."

"Drugs?" Brunelle spat. "This was about drugs?"

"About *running* drugs," Montero corrected. "Apparently she was looking to establish a distribution partner up here in Seattle. She said she had an excuse to travel up here regularly, some Brazilian karate thing."

"Capoeira," Brunelle offered.

"Right. Whatever." Montero shrugged. "She played mule and brought a few balloons of heroin up here in her colon. Then she looked for someone who could sell it for her."

"Nguyen," Brunelle surmised.

"No." Montero shook her head. "Ostrander. She just knew him as 'Pete,' but her description matches. That's why he had her name in his pocket. But she didn't give him her real name, just that Brazilian nickname."

"Portuguese," Brunelle corrected.

"Whatever."

"So, she didn't have anything to do with the Ostrander murder at all?" Brunelle was wracked with a pang of guilt that Chen had been shot for absolutely nothing.

"I didn't say that," Montero responded. "She was asking around the International District for someone to move the drugs, with a promise of more. She settled on Ostrander because he was the first to say yes, but plenty of people heard about what she was doing. She said some Asian guy confronted her on the sidewalk and offered to be her connection. Again, her description matched Nguyen: young, thin, really tall. She told him she'd already offered it to Ostrander, but she could be convinced to change that. She didn't care. She just wanted the money. Apparently, her life in Rio is pretty rough. She was just looking to make a better life."

"The American dream," Brunelle quipped. "Getting rich off the misfortune of others."

Montero laughed darkly. "That is kind of the American dream, isn't it? Or part of it. Hell, you and I make a living because bad shit happens to other people."

"I'd be willing to get laid off," Brunelle answered. "If it meant people stopped shooting each other over shit-covered bags of drugs."

"Balloons," Montero corrected. "They're sturdier and pass easily."

"Good to know," Brunelle replied. "Something to keep in mind next time I go to Brazil."

"You've been to Brazil?"

"Nope," Brunelle answered. "But maybe I can sneak some Adderall into Vancouver or something."

Montero smiled weakly and nodded, but didn't reply immediately.

"How's he doing?" Brunelle asked. That's what they really cared about anyway.

Montero shook her head. "The doctors said it could go either way. The bullets missed his heart and lungs, but they tore up his intestines pretty good. The biggest risk is sepsis. The next forty-eight hours are critical."

Brunelle ran his hands over his head. "I shouldn't have called him so late. You guys could have grabbed her when she went out for coffee the next morning. Case the hotel or something."

Brunelle wanted Montero to wave away the hindsight, but instead she shrugged and agreed. "Yeah, that would have been safer. But then again, we thought she was a witness. There was no way for us to know she'd open fire."

"Still," Brunelle said.

"Yeah," Montero agreed.

"So, does this help the case against Nguyen at all?" Montero asked. "Was it worth it?"

"I don't know if it was worth it," Brunelle answered. "But, yeah, it helps."

"Enough?"

Brunelle shrugged. "I don't know. At least I know what really happened that night. It's always better to know the truth. I almost forgot that."

"So, what's next?" Montero asked.

Brunelle picked up Montero's report again. "I give a copy of the truth to Nguyen's attorney. Then I wait to see how he twists it."

CHAPTER 29

To Brunelle's surprise, Welles didn't try to twist the truth of the relationships between Jeremy Nguyen, Peter Ostrander, and Maria Oliveira. To the contrary, he appeared to ignore it. Brunelle forwarded him Montero's original report, as well as all the supplemental reports about Chen's shooting, Maria's arrest, and Montero's interrogation. He sent a hard copy via courier, and a digital copy via email. But Welles never replied. Not even so much as a 'Received' email.

So when the morning of trial arrived, Brunelle wondered what Welles had planned. Maybe the defense attorney had calculated that letting the jury know the victim was an aspiring drug trafficker would increase the chances of an acquittal. Or maybe Welles just wasn't all that surprised. After all, his client would have known all of that firsthand, and would almost certainly have told his attorney. As Brunelle entered the courtroom early for that first morning of preliminary housekeeping matters, he found Welles already there, awaiting the arrival of his client from the jail and appearing, by any measure, calm. Relaxed even.

Meckle hadn't arrived yet, but Peter Ostrander's parents had. They were seated toward the back of the gallery. They looked like they knew they were supposed to be there, but didn't know exactly why. The truth was, nothing too interesting happened on the first day of trial. Preliminary things, mostly. Ruling on admissibility of evidence. Lawyer stuff. It could be pretty boring. He checked in with them and told them as much. But parents of a murder victim usually want to watch the entire trial, and they told him as much. He thanked them for coming, then made his way to his (he had to admit) worthy opponent.

"Good morning," Brunelle walked up to the defense table where Welles was seated. "Ready to go? Your guy could still plead guilty, you know."

"And why in the world would he do that?" Welles replied with a roll of his eyes. "He'd be no better off than if he tried the case and lost. And I daresay, when we try this case, the most likely outcome will not be a conviction, but rather a resounding and decisive acquittal."

Brunelle rolled his own eyes. Even with no one else in the courtroom yet, Welles talked like he was auditioning for a Shakespeare play.

"I don't know," Brunelle replied. "You got those new reports, right? I think that lays out a pretty clear motive for your guy. I liked the love triangle story, but rival drug dealers? Way better. They may hate my victim, but they'll hate your guy at least as much."

Welles cocked his head and offered a confused expression. "You expect to introduce any of that at trial? This trial? Now?"

"Well, yeah," Brunelle answered. "Of course. It's motive evidence."

"I don't know about that," Welles scoffed. "But I do know it's late discovery. You can't dump thirty pages of reports on me a week before trial. Well, you can, and you did, but only for information purposes. It's not admissible at trial. I've had no opportunity to investigate any of the claims in those reports."

"You've had a week," Brunelle defended.

"Yes, one week. And my client is looking at thirty years in prison." Welles laughed lightly. "Oh, no, Mr. Brunelle. There is no way you get to change the entire theory of your case at the last moment. It simply isn't fair."

"It's the truth," Brunelle pointed out.

But Welles just laughed again. "Irrelevant."

Brunelle retreated to his counsel table and considered Welles's position as the courtroom filled one by one with the other participants in the trial. The bailiff, the court reporter, the defendant and his guards, and finally the young, up-and-coming, whiz kid prosecutor. Oh wait. It was just Meckle.

"Uh, hey, Dave," he said as he arrived at their table. "I thought we said we'd walk down together from the office."

"Did we?" Brunelle asked. He honestly didn't remember that. He kind of didn't care either. He was still thinking about what Welles had said—and what he was going to say to the judge when that last participant entered the courtroom. "Sorry. Got a lot on my mind."

Of course, of course," Meckle accepted the explanation. "Me too, right? First big murder trial. Here we go, huh?"

Brunelle half-frowned. "Sure. Here we go."

And there they went, as Judge Tillerson entered the courtroom to his bailiff's bellow and ascended to his perch over the proceedings, and all the other participants.

"Are the parties ready for trial," he asked formally, "in the matter of the State of Washington versus Jeremy Nguyen?"

Welles broke protocol to answer first. "The defense is ready, Your Honor."

But part of the reason he was able to speak first was that Brunelle was still thinking. About what Welles had said. And about what he better say to the judge, right away.

"I believe there may be an issue we need to deal with," Brunelle informed Judge Tillerson, "before we proceed too far."

"Issue?" Judge Tillerson frowned. "What sort of issue?"

"An evidence issue, I suppose," Brunelle offered. "There's new evidence in the case. I provided it to defense counsel last week, but apparently he's going to move to suppress it."

Tillerson sighed. "Mr. Welles, is that accurate?"

"The part about new evidence is accurate," Welles acknowledged. "But I wouldn't categorize it as a motion to suppress on my part. It's more of a motion by the State to violate my client's rights to a speedy trial and prepared counsel by admitting prejudicially late information."

"A motion to violate the defendant's Constitutional rights?" Brunelle asked with a barely concealed snarl. "Really?"

Welles nodded, deadpan. "I imagine the Prosecutor's Office has a template for that."

"Alright, enough," Tillerson interjected. "Mr. Brunelle what's the nature of this evidence?"

So, Brunelle explained. About Joaninha. About Chen. About the real motive for the shooting.

"So, all that stuff you said at the hearing on Mr. Welles's motion to dismiss?" Judge Tillerson asked when he'd finished. "That stuff about a love triangle and jealousy as the motive? That wasn't accurate?"

"Apparently not," Brunelle admitted. "Although I was right that it had something to do with that note in the victim's pocket. I just misread the name."

Tillerson pursed his lips and nodded a few times, then turned to Welles. "And you're objecting to this new evidence?"

"I'm not objecting to it, per se," Welles answered. "It exists or it doesn't. But I do object to its use in this trial. The trial that's supposed to start today. The trial that I and my client have prepared for. The trial Mr. Brunelle deceived us into thinking we'd be trying."

"I didn't deceive anyone," Brunelle protested.

But the judge cut him off. "Please refrain from arguing directly at each other," he reminded them. "Direct your comments to the bench." Then, "I don't think you deceived the defense, Mr. Brunelle. Not intentionally, which is what deceive means, I think. But you certainly misled the defense. And the Court. This is not the case you represented it was."

"Well, I don't know about that, Your Honor," Brunelle disagreed. "Mr. Nguyen still shot and killed Mr. Ostrander. The exact reason—the motive—isn't something I actually have to prove. It just helps put the act into context."

"If you don't actually have to prove it," Tillerson questioned, "then why should I let you change it at the last second? I mean, if it's not that big of a deal."

"I didn't say it wasn't a big deal," Brunelle defended.

"But if it is a big deal," Tillerson challenged. "then isn't it an even bigger deal to change it at the last second? Doesn't that prejudice the defense?"

Brunelle took a moment to take a deep breath and collect his thoughts. "I can't help the fact that this information was only recently discovered. I turned it over to the defense as soon as I received it. The same day, even. But, Your Honor, it's the truth. And if the truth is prejudicial to the defendant, then so be it. His remedy should be additional time to investigate that truth and figure out how to respond to it, not suppression of that truth from the jury.

"Because a trial is a quest for the truth?" Tillerson offered.

"Yes," Brunelle answered.

"May I be heard, Your Honor?" Welles interjected. Judge Tillerson assented with a nod, and he continued. "This isn't about the truth. It's about fairness. And it is fundamentally unfair to charge a man with murder, hold him in custody pending his trial, wax eloquent about some fantastical love triangle at the motion to dismiss, hold him in custody even longer, then on the eve of trial, abandon the case theory that allowed the case to stay alive and dump a brand new theory on the defense, with no time to properly investigate or rebut this new theory which, one can now imagine, might be totally thrown out again in a few weeks if Mr. Brunelle suddenly discovered some new motive to attach to my client's actions. Perhaps a contested inheritance from a reclusive uncle, or a chance to recover an ancient artifact of untold power from the wilds of the Sahara Desert? You want the truth? The truth is: that's not fair. It's not Constitutional. And it shouldn't be allowed."

Judge Tillerson sat in silence for several seconds as he considered the argument. Finally, he nodded and looked down to Brunelle.

"I have to agree with Mr. Welles," he said. "A criminal trial isn't about the truth—it's about what the State can prove, in court, beyond a reasonable doubt. It's about the presumption of innocence, and the right to remain silent, and the right to a speedy and public trial. The right to prepared counsel. All of those cut against the truth, or at least make the truth an irrelevant luxury. It doesn't matter if someone committed the crime; it matters if you can prove it. If you can't, they're not guilty. Period. Even if they are guilty. That doesn't sound like truth to me. It sounds like procedure, and safeguards, and holding the government to its burden to prove every element of a crime beyond a reasonable doubt before a person is deprived of their liberty."

Brunelle didn't respond. He knew there was no point.

"But that isn't just what I think," Tillerson went on. "That's also what the Court of Appeals thinks, and the Supreme Court. If I let you put on this evidence, Mr. Brunelle, evidence divulged to the defense only one week before a first-degree murder trial, it won't matter how many times the jury says Mr. Nguyen is guilty—you could give them a hundred verdict forms to sign—the conviction would never stand up on appeal. At best, it'd be remanded for a new trial. At worst, the conviction would be vacated and dismissed. Is that what you want?"

Brunelle shook his head. "No, Your Honor."

"Do you want to try this case twice?" Tillerson continued.

"No, Your Honor," Brunelle answered. "I want to try it once, in a month or two, after Mr. Welles has had a chance to fully investigate the new evidence. That way the jury can get the truth, regardless of procedure and safeguards. I think if you asked the jurors, they'd want the truth above all else."

Tillerson surrendered a small grin. "Maybe. But this 'issue' isn't in front of them. It's in front of me. And I don't get to simply render a verdict and go home. I have to protect the rights of the accused along the way to that verdict. I'm sorry, Mr. Brunelle, but there's no way I can let you introduce such late evidence in your case-in-chief."

Brunelle let his shoulders drop and sighed. "So, what am I supposed to do exactly, Your Honor? It's not like I can put on evidence of my original theory—the love triangle. There's no discovery violation, but I know it's not true. I can't put on evidence I know isn't true. But the evidence I know is true, you just suppressed."

Tillerson's expression hardened. "I'm going to state my ruling one more time, Mr. Brunelle. The State may not introduce any of this late evidence in its case-in-chief. Period. Do you understand my ruling?"

Brunelle nodded weakly. "Yes, Your Honor."

"Are you sure, Mr. Brunelle?" Tillerson persisted. "Are you sure you understand it completely?"

"Yes, Your Honor," Brunelle assured.

Tillerson narrowed his eyes and regarded Brunelle from on high. "I hope so, Mr. Brunelle."

With that settled, the judge took a moment to think, then announced, "In light of this development, I am going to adjourn the trial for one day, in order to give Mr. Brunelle some opportunity to determine how to proceed. We will reconvene tomorrow morning at the same time."

"I would object to that, Your Honor," Welles spoke up. "This isn't something Mr. Brunelle couldn't have anticipated. In fact, he should have known the Court would never admit evidence turned over so late in such a serious case. I have to believe he was prepared for the Court's ruling."

"I probably should have been," Brunelle agreed, "but I got all caught up in that whole truth thing. I guess I expected that to carry the day."

"Careful, Mr. Brunelle," Judge Tillerson warned. "You're getting close to maligning the Court. We all have jobs to do, and I'm doing mine." Then he turned to Welles. "One day will not prejudice the defendant, Mr. Welles. I will see everyone here first thing tomorrow morning."

He banged his gavel to signal both his ruling and the lack of any further opportunity to argue with it. Then, just to be sure, the judge departed the bench and retired to his chambers.

Welles sat down and entered into a hushed conference with his client. Brunelle remained standing, his brain still trying to figure out how to proceed without being able to tell the jury why Nguyen shot Ostrander.

Meckle stood up and interrupted his thoughts. "Do you want to talk strategy?"

"Nope," Brunelle snapped, without even looking at his co-counsel. Instead he turned and marched out of the courtroom, past the reporters and even the victim's parents without saying a word.

There was only one person Brunelle wanted to talk to right then, even if he couldn't talk back.

CHAPTER 30

Brunelle had been to Harborview Medical Center before, of course. Plenty of times. But not like this. Those times were professional, detached. This was professional too, but also personal, and anything but detached.

Chen had been moved out of Intensive Care but was still listed in serious condition. Because he wasn't family, Brunelle had to wait for visiting hours, and even then had to convince the lead shift nurse to let him go into Chen's room. Non-family visitors weren't exactly encouraged for non-responsive patients, and Chen still hadn't come fully out of the drug-induced coma they'd put him in while they tried to prevent his body from shutting down from the deadly combination of shrapnel and sepsis.

"Soon," the nurse had assured after he asked when Chen might come out of it. "Very soon, in fact. Maybe you should come back tomorrow."

But Brunelle was going to be busy 'tomorrow.' He needed today. He needed to say something, even if his friend didn't hear it.

"I'm sorry," he whispered over Chen's motionless body. The detective was hooked up to an I.V. and more machines than Brunelle felt like counting. Screens displayed his heart rate and oxygen levels and God knew what else. But Brunelle's gaze was fixed on the closed eyes of his friend. "I'm really, really sorry."

He took a moment, then added the worst part. "And it was all for nothing. We finally figured out who 'Joan Inha' was. *You* guys did. You and Montero. You finally figured out the motive, and it wasn't what we thought it was at all. It wasn't what *I* thought it was. It's better. So much better. Because it's true. And you took a bullet for us to find out the truth, but it doesn't matter because the judge isn't going to let me tell the jury anyway. You guys did it, and I can't do anything with it anyway. It was all for nothing."

Brunelle looked up and out the window, his eyes resting on nothing in particular as his own thoughts overran his mind.

"When this is all over," he rasped, as he lowered his eyes again to his bedridden friend, "I hope you can forgive me."

Chen's eyes didn't open, but his lips parted just enough to croak, "Don't apologize. And don't make excuses."

"Larry!" Brunelle grabbed Chen's hand, a little too roughly, he realized as cables and tubes were sent shaking.

Chen managed a slight squeeze back on Brunelle's hand. "I was doing my job," he wheezed. "Now go do yours."

CHAPTER 31

The next morning came quickly enough and found all the same players in the courtroom. Welles whispering with his client. Meckle waiting for Brunelle to arrive. Mr. and Mrs. Ostrander seated in the gallery. Brunelle checked in with them, then made his way to the prosecution table.

"Are we ready?' Meckle asked. It seemed genuine, like he really didn't know.

Brunelle nodded. "We're ready. We have a job to do."

That job, preliminarily at least, was a lot of procedure and little substance. The judge took the bench, confirmed the prosecution was ready to go, and then off they went. It took the better part of the day, but they managed to resolve the few remaining evidentiary issues, and select a jury of twelve, plus two alternates, from a pool of sixty prospective jurors. Once they were sworn in, the judge gave the attorneys a fifteen-minute break before opening statements. He was determined to keep the trial moving.

Brunelle was going to give the opening statement. And if there had been any doubt about that, it was resolved as he and Meckle discussed the difficulties the State faced in that particular case.

"Are you going to mention self-defense in your opening?" Meckle asked Brunelle, both men standing next to the counsel table, but too nervous to sit.

Brunelle nodded at the question. "That's the conundrum, isn't it? It reminds me of this book I had when I was a kid. It was called 'Fortunately, Unfortunately' or something like that. All these things happen to this kid, some good, some bad, and for each one, it would start, 'Fortunately, there a haystack to land in… Unfortunately, there was a needle in the haystack…' That's what it's like here."

He pointed to the jury box. "On the one hand, self-defense isn't actually an element of the offense, so I'm not required to mention it in my opening. On the other hand, it's a complete defense to the charge, so I probably shouldn't ignore it. On another hand, we can block the defendant's statement to Montero if we just don't ask her about it, so maybe there won't be any evidence of self-defense, and I shouldn't be the one to raise it. On another hand, even if we don't introduce it, the defendant could always take the stand after we rest and tell the jury it was self-defense, but I can't mention whether a defendant might or might not testify because that would be a comment on his right to remain silent. On another hand, if I do address self-defense, I'm boxing Welles in to a specific defense and that might be burden-shifting. On another hand, if I don't mention self-defense at all, but Welles does in his opening, then they'll think I was hiding it, or worse, they'll think Welles knows more than I do."

"That's a lot of hands," Meckle observed.

"It sure is," Brunelle agreed. "So, tell me. What would you do?"

Meckle smiled weakly. "I'd let you do the opening."

Judge Tillerson reentered the courtroom then and once he'd taken his spot on the bench, he confirmed both sides were ready. They were, and the bailiff fetched the jury. Once the jurors were also in the courtroom and comfortably seated in the jury box, Judge Tillerson spoke.

"Ladies and gentlemen of the jury, please give your attention to Mr. Brunelle, who will deliver the opening statement on behalf of the State."

CHAPTER 32

Brunelle stood up and stepped out from behind the prosecution counsel table. He buttoned his suit coat and made his way to the center of the well, directly in front of the center of the jury box. He stood one step too close, too close for a speaker anyway. But he was more than a speaker. He was a lawyer, a prosecutor. He didn't just need them to listen, he needed them to feel. He needed them to engage. So he pushed, just slightly, into their bubble, then waited just a little too long before finally speaking.

"Self-defense. There, I said it. This is a case about self-defense. Or rather," he paused and raised a single professorial finger, "it's a case about the absence of self-defense. It's a case about what is not self-defense. It's a case," another pause, "about murder."

Brunelle took a step back. He had them engaged. Now he needed them to listen. And understand. And believe.

He pointed over to the defendant. "That man over there, the defendant, Jeremy Nguyen, shot and killed Peter Ostrander in the early morning hours, underneath a freeway overpass in the International District. He shot him twice. Once through the chest, and once right between the eyes. Dead center. Dead. Center."

Brunelle paused again, not just for the effect on the listeners, but to gather his thoughts. Tillerson really had cut his feet out from under him. This was the point in the opening statement where he would normally step back and tell the story, the victim's story. Introduce him to the jury, humanize him, then explain how he came to find himself in the situation that led to his violent death at the hands of another.

This was where he would admit that Peter Ostrander had some criminal history. Drugs. Drug possession. But he was ready to branch out to drug selling. Not great, but true. Real. And not uncommon. People needed money to buy their drugs, and it was a slippery slope from sharing with friends, to making friends reimburse you for the cost, to outright selling at a profit. Peter Ostrander was no saint, but neither was Jeremy Nguyen.

Jeremy Nguyen was following a similar life path. From small-time drug user to small-time drug dealer. But he was an ambitious small-time drug dealer. And he saw an opportunity to jump to the big-time, with a pipeline from South America. Never mind that it was a visiting Brazilian martial artist who probably didn't have much more of a business plan than he did, let alone an established supply chain back home. He saw a brass ring and he was going to grab for it. It was a business decision, a risk, a hope wrapped in a dream. Just like whoever invented the pet rock. Even ridiculous ideas could be successful.

The only thing standing in Jeremy Nguyen's way was a rival small-time drug dealer who wanted to grab that same brass ring, ridiculous or not. And so, there was a showdown. And when there's a showdown between drug dealers, even small-time drug dealers, the odds were good that one of them wouldn't come out alive.

Peter Ostrander paid the price for his ambition. He was armed, but he never fired his gun. He never got the chance. Because Jeremy Nguyen shot him first. Killed him. Murdered him. With a shot between the eyes. Dead center.

But Brunelle couldn't say any of that. Nothing about Joaninha the drug mule, or Joan Inha the love interest. Nothing about the motive. Nothing about the why.

So he had to talk about the what.

"Peter Ostrander can't tell you what happened that night. He can't tell you because he's dead. From a bullet that entered his skull just above the bridge of his nose, then ricocheted off the inside of his skull and tore his brain apart. A bullet fired by Jeremy Nguyen.

"But even though Peter isn't here to tell his story, there are others who can speak for him, based on the physical evidence left behind. You are going to hear from a series of expert witnesses who will explain to you several very important facts."

Brunelle raised his hands in front of him to count off those facts.

"First, Peter never fired a gun. He was found faceup on the pavement of the parking lot, a handgun a few inches from his outstretched hand. But a ballistics expert will explain to you that the gun was still fully loaded, an evidence technician will explain to you that no casings were recovered at the scene that were linked to Peter's gun, and the medical examiner will explain that a chemical test administered to Peter's hands confirmed that he never fired a gun.

"Second, the shots which the defendant fired and which ended Peter Ostrander's life were fired from a distance, at least eighteen inches away. There was no struggle for a gun. There was space between them and the defendant took his time to aim and deliver that perfect kill shot.

"Third, after murdering Peter Ostrander, after shooting him in the head under a freeway overpass at one in the morning, the defendant fled the scene. He didn't attempt to render aid; he didn't alert anyone at a nearby restaurant or business; and he certainly didn't call 911. He fled. He went home and hid. If it hadn't been for the fact that the owner of the restaurant across the street happened to hear the shots and run out to see the make, model, and license plate of the vehicle the defendant fled in, he might never have been identified. Peter Ostrander might have ended up as just another cold case. A man, clearly murdered, left for dead, his killer escaped into the night never to be identified. Never to be found. Never to be held accountable."

Another pause, combined with a pensive look down and a step to one side. Then, a look up again to the jurors.

"But he was identified. He was found. And now it is time to hold him accountable. It's time for *you* to hold him accountable. Listen closely to the evidence. Draw reasonable inferences from it. Determine what really happened that night. And when you do, you will determine that this was not a case of self-defense. This was a case of murder.

"And at the end of this trial, I will stand up before you again and ask you to find Jeremy Nguyen guilty of the first-degree murder of Peter Ostrander. Thank you."

Brunelle returned to his seat and Meckle gave him a whispered "Good job" which he ignored. Not cool to look happy in front of the jury. He needed to look serious, focused on justice; not chummy, focused on praise.

"Thank you, Mr. Brunelle," Judge Tillerson took a moment to say before instructing the jury as to their next task. "Now, ladies and gentlemen, please give your attention to Mr. Welles, who will deliver the opening statement on behalf of the defendant."

CHAPTER 33

Welles stood up and nodded to the judge. "Thank you, Your Honor."

He stepped around his own counsel table and offered more nods: another to Tillerson, one to Brunelle and Meckle, and finally to the jury. "May it please the Court, counsel, members of the jury. I am William Harrison Welles and I have the honor of representing Mr. Jeremy Nguyen. So, let me say it too:

"Self-defense.

"There, I said it too.

"Mr. Brunelle said it. And now I've said it. But do you know who said it first?"

He, too, turned and pointed at his client. "Mr. Jeremy Nguyen did. That very night. When he turned himself in to the police and they asked him what happened, he told them. Self-defense. That's what he said because that's what happened."

Welles knew how to use a pause as well. He took a moment to let his introduction sink in, turning and pacing a few steps, before stopping and addressing the jurors again with a second introduction.

"Self-defense," he repeated. Then he expanded. "The lawful use of force. Lawful force. Now, let me say that again. Lawful force. That may seem like a strange concept, I realize. A contradiction even. An anachronism in our modern world of safe spaces and candlelight vigils. And I don't mean to disparage such things. Overall, the evolution of our society to one where violence is a last resort rather than a first resort has been a good thing, a positive development in the arc of our civilization. But do not forget: even if it's no longer a first resort, lawful force is still a last resort.

"You still have the right to defend yourself."

Another gesture toward his client.

"*Mr. Nguyen* had the right to defend himself."

Welles paced slowly back to his original standing spot. Just like Brunelle, he gravitated to the spot directly in front of the center of the jury box. Unlike Brunelle, though, he remained just a little too close to them. He didn't want them comfortable. Comfortable juries were complacent, compliant juries. Compliant juries rubber-stamped the charges put to them by the prosecutor. But uncomfortable juries were questioning juries, and questioning juries acquitted. Maybe.

"Now, you just heard Mr. Brunelle's opening statement. He told you what some of the witnesses are going to say. He complained about what the witnesses weren't going to say. But what he didn't really tell you is what happened. What did happen that night?"

Welles looked over at the prosecution table and gestured at Brunelle. "They don't know."

He turned back to the jurors. "Ladies and gentlemen, they don't know. They don't know what happened. But there is one person who does know. One person who can tell you exactly what happened and why. The person who told the police that very night what happened. Mr. Nguyen. He told the police it was self-defense. And he's going to tell you that too."

Brunelle tried not to raise an eyebrow at that, let alone a full-on spit take. Welles had just promised the defendant was going to testify. Defense attorneys never did that—or at least, they were supposed to never do that. They taught that at the defense attorney seminars. But the jurors didn't know that, so there was no reason for Brunelle to allow them to see his surprise. And there was no reason for Welles to hold back.

He pointed to the witness stand. "Mr. Nguyen is going to sit in that witness chair right there, and he is going to tell you exactly what happened that fateful morn. He is going to raise his right hand, and he's going to swear to tell the truth, the whole truth, and nothing but the truth, and he's going to tell you the same thing he tried to tell the detectives that night. He was defending himself."

Welles could check another thing off on his fingers as well.

"He used lawful force.

"To defend himself.

"Against an armed assailant.

"In an abandoned parking lot.

"In the dark of the wee hours.

"Under a deafening freeway overpass."

Welles took another moment, then nodded several times, partially to himself, mostly to the jury.

"Mr. Nguyen isn't proud of what he had to do that night, ladies and gentlemen. In fact, he wishes it had never happened. He wishes he had never been put in that position. But wishes are for birthday cakes and magic fountains. The truth of the matter is, he was put in that position. He had to make a split-second decision, based on all the factors he was confronted with. He made the decision. He made the right decision. He made the lawful decision."

Welles turned and walked back to the defense table, but rather than sit down, he stood behind Nguyen and placed his hands on his client's shoulders.

"Mr. Nguyen will live with that decision for the rest of his life. But he will do so knowing he had no other choice. At the end of this trial, you too will have a decision to make. But you will also know exactly what to do. Yes, Mr. Nguyen was forced to take Mr. Ostrander's life that terrible, terrible night, but he did not commit murder. He used lawful force. And that, ladies and gentlemen, means he is not guilty.

"Thank you all for your attention, and I look forward to speaking with you again at the end of the trial."

Brunelle wasn't sure about the rest of Welles's opening, but he knew that last sentence was true. Welles loved the sound of his own voice. He had spoken longer than Brunelle, but in truth, neither of them had really told the jury what had happened. Not really. Not the details. Yes, Nguyen shot and killed Ostrander. But beyond that? Well, Brunelle supposed that would depend on what the witnesses actually ended up saying.

That thought dovetailed precisely with Judge Tillerson's next declaration: "The State may call its first witness."

Brunelle stayed seated as Meckle stood to announce, "The State calls Susan Ostrander."

CHAPTER 34

Susan Ostrander was, of course, the victim's mother. Someone had to identify the victim and remind the jury that, prior to the acts of the defendant, the victim had been a living, breathing human being. From a purely practical perspective, it was an element of the offense. From a more strategic perspective, they wanted the jury to actually care, at least a little bit, that Peter Ostrander—a person none of them had ever met—was dead. If they didn't care, why would they convict? It wasn't sufficient for the conviction, but it was necessary. And who better to make them care than Mom?

It also provided Brunelle the opportunity to give Meckle some witnesses to examine. The only thing worse than having a second-chair taking up space next to him the entire trial would be to have him take up space and not do anything. The jury would wonder why Meckle was there at all. And they would wonder what kind of narcissistic jerk Brunelle was for making him sit there the whole trial but not letting him do any of the work. So Meckle got to do the first witness, and the one with the biggest emotional punch. And there was pretty much no way he could screw it up.

"Could you please state your name for the record?" Meckle began after Mrs. Ostrander was sworn in.

She answered the question easily enough, although she was pale and drawn. Exactly as the jury might expect. Meckle led her through the basics: she was Peter Ostrander's mother; she hadn't seen him for a few weeks prior to the murder; she didn't think anything about it because he was a grown man now; and one morning, shortly after breakfast, she received a visit from a Detective Chen who informed her that her son had been murdered.

Brunelle wasn't worried Meckle would do anything wrong. They'd discussed his questions in advance. She would identify Peter from an in-life photograph taken before his murder, from his birthday party the previous summer. She would not be shown any of the crime scene or autopsy photos. And then she would be done.

The only variable was what Welles would do. But Brunelle had a pretty good idea of that too. Unfortunately.

"Thank you, Mrs. Ostrander," Meckle concluded his direct examination. "I don't have any further questions."

Judge Tillerson looked down at the defense table. "Cross-examination, Mr. Welles?"

What do you ask the grieving mother of a murder victim?

Absolutely nothing.

"No questions, Your Honor," Welles informed the Court. "Thank you."

Brunelle frowned inside. Not only did Welles know how to talk; he knew when to shut up.

"Call your next witness," Tillerson instructed Brunelle and Meckle as soon as Susan Ostrander stepped down from the witness stand. Mom had been a good first witness. She set the tone, but it was time to present the case in earnest. And Welles was unlikely to let any further witnesses pass unchallenged.

It was Meckle's turn again. "The State calls Timothy Han," he announced.

They were starting simple. Telling the story in the same way it unfolded for the cops. It put the jury in the place of the investigators, making them feel more invested in its resolution. At least that was the theory. But

Brunelle wasn't the only one who'd studied the theory of trial practice. Welles knew a thing or two about trying a case. And one of those things or two was to be absolutely surgical in cross-examination. Minimalist, even. Brunelle had hoped Welles would just do the long rambling, 'let me re-ask you everything the State already asked you, so you can tell the jury the State's theory of the case again' type of cross-exam. But he knew better. When Meckle had finished eliciting Han's observations that night—about the gunshots, about the man running across the parking lot, about the car he drove away in—it was Welles's turn to cross examine.

Brunelle had learned somewhere that, in public speaking anyway, if you wanted an audience to remember something, you should break it down into three subpoints. Everyone can remember three subpoints. But beyond three, it became difficult; the more subpoints, the more difficult. Brunelle wasn't sure if Welles had learned the same thing along the way, but he did notice that Welles only had three questions for the man who identified his client as the shooter.

First question. "My client," he pointed again at Nguyen, "is the man you saw running away from the alleged victim that morning, correct?"

Han looked again at Nguyen, seated at the defense table in a suit and tie. "Yes. I believe so."

Second question. "You came outside after the sound of gunshots, correct?"

"Yes," Han answered. "That's why I came outside."

Third question. "So, you didn't see all the things that led up to my client having to defend himself and shoot the other man in self-defense, correct?"

Part question, part speech. But Han still had to answer it.

"I didn't see what happened before the gunshots," he admitted.

"No further questions," Welles announced.

The next witness was Seattle Police Officer Raymond Giraldi, a young athletic cop and the first officer on scene. Brunelle handled that direct exam, if only to break things up a bit. Giraldi didn't do anything except observe the body and know enough to back the hell up and call the homicide guys. He said it better than that on the stand, of course, but when Brunelle finished his direct exam, Welles stood up again with another three questions for the officer.

"It took you four minutes to arrive at the scene after the 911 call came in, correct?"

"Yes, sir," Giraldi answered formally.

"Before you arrived, the crime scene was not secure and could have been compromised by someone entering it and disturbing whatever physical evidence might have been deposited there, correct?"

"It's possible, sir," Giraldi admitted. "Unlikely, I think, given what time it was, but it is possible, yes, sir."

And finally, "You are a patrol officer, not an evidence collection technician, correct?"

"Yes, sir," Giraldi confirmed.

Welles nodded, then looked up and informed the judge he had no further questions. To whatever extent Brunelle was worried that Welles's *de minimus* cross-examination might have been effective, he knew he wouldn't need to worry about Welles only asking three surgical questions of their next witness.

"The State," he announced, "calls Detective Julia Montero."

CHAPTER 35

Det. Montero had been waiting in the hallway, but she didn't make it three steps into the courtroom before Welles stood up and addressed the Court.

"Your Honor," he said, "before the detective testifies, I have a motion."

Montero stopped halfway down the walkway to the witness stand. Brunelle sighed and stood up. Tillerson raised an eyebrow.

"A motion?" he asked.

"Yes, Your Honor," Welles confirmed, "and I'd like it heard outside the presence of the jury."

Another sigh from Brunelle. And Montero. And Tillerson.

The problem with asking to have a motion heard outside the presence of the jury was that it was difficult to explain, with the jury listening, why it needed to be heard without them listening. That meant there was really only one thing the judge could do.

"Okay," Tillerson acquiesced. He looked to the jurors. "Ladies and gentlemen, I'm going to ask you to retire to the jury room for a few minutes while I speak with the attorneys."

There was a surprised but compliant murmur from the jury box as the jurors stood up and followed the bailiff into the jury room. When the door clicked shut behind them, Judge Tillerson turned to Welles. "What is the issue, Mr. Welles? And why couldn't this have been addressed prior to opening statements? I am not going to constantly interrupt the trial with arguments outside the presence of the jury."

"Of course, Your Honor," Welles inclined his head deferentially. "And I assure Your Honor that I have no intention of using motions like this or otherwise to disrupt the flow of Mr. Brunelle's case."

I doubt that, Brunelle thought.

"I don't need to," Welles continued. "His case is spotty and disjointed enough on its own."

Ah. Brunelle frowned. *There it is.*

"What's your motion, Mr. Welles?" Judge Tillerson directed.

"Yes, Your Honor," Welles acknowledged. "Of course, Your Honor. It's very simple, Your Honor. It pertains to Detective Montero."

"Yes, I assumed that," Tillerson said. "What is the motion?"

"I intend to cross-examine Detective Montero on the fact that she was not the lead detective on the case and how that impacts her knowledge of the case," Welles explained. "But I do not believe the State should be allowed to tell the jury about what happened to Detective Chen, as it would tend to invoke sympathy for law enforcement generally, and the officers on this case specifically."

"So, you want to tell the jury that Detective Chen should be testifying instead of Detective Montero," Tillerson clarified, "but you don't want them to know why he's not testifying. Is that right?"

"Yes, essentially," Welles confirmed.

Tillerson turned to the prosecution. "Any response, Mr. Brunelle?"

"Uh, yeah," Brunelle nodded, "I have a response. Mr. Welles has a choice to make. He can either attack Detective Montero for not being the lead detective and open the door to why Detective Chen isn't here, or he can back off, let Detective Montero testify, and we don't need to talk about what happened to Detective Chen."

"So, you weren't planning," the judge questioned, "on having Detective Montero explain why Detective Chen won't be testifying?"

Brunelle thought for a moment. "Well, yeah, I was probably going to ask her that," he admitted. "The jury would probably want to know why the lead detective isn't here."

"This is exactly why I made my motion before Detective Montero took the witness stand," Welles interjected. "I anticipated Mr. Brunelle would attempt to use this situation to back-door his last-minute theory about this being some sort of drug-running murder."

"I'm not back-dooring anything," Brunelle insisted. "I'm just explaining something the jury is naturally going to want explained."

"Like the motive for the killing?" Tillerson challenged. "I don't think that's the test, Mr. Brunelle."

"Maybe not," Brunelle admitted, "but I don't think we should not tell the jury anything at all. They might think he was fired or disciplined or quit or just doesn't care."

"Well, now," Welles spoke up, "we can't help what the jury might speculate about."

"So, we can tell them why Detective Chen isn't here after all?" Tillerson asked him. "You're withdrawing your motion?"

"I am not." Welles stiffened his back.

"Yeah, I didn't think so," Tillerson replied. "So, here's what we're going to do. Mr. Brunelle, you can tell the jury Detective Chen isn't here because he was injured in the line of duty. If you do anything more than that, I will declare a mistrial, and we will schedule Mr. Welles's inevitable motion to dismiss for governmental misconduct. And Mr. Welles, you can explore how Detective Montero might have less information than Detective Chen, but if you make any suggestion that Detective Chen's absence is voluntary or due to any sort of malfeasance, I will open up the entire issue of the shooting, and Mr. Brunelle can present all of that late motive evidence he dumped on you last week."

He took a moment to let his ruling sink in. "Mr. Brunelle, understood?"

Brunelle nodded. "Yes, Your Honor."

"Mr. Welles, understood?"

Welles surrendered one curt nod himself. "Understood, Your Honor."

"Good," Tillerson said. "Now, bring in the jury."

The bailiff executed the judge's command and after a few minutes of shuffling, mumbling, sitting, walking, swearing in, and sitting again, Brunelle was ready to begin his direct examination of Det. Montero. Brunelle, not Meckle. She was way too important of a witness. And it was Brunelle's turn anyway.

Too bad it wouldn't be more impressive. The problem with a lead detective testifying was that they usually couldn't really testify to all that much. The jury expected to hear from them—and would assume the worst if they weren't called as a witness—but in truth, their job was to assign jobs to everyone else. They didn't collect the evidence; the evidence techs did that. They didn't test fire the firearms; the ballistics experts did that. They didn't conduct the autopsy; the medical examiner did that. Although they usually observed the autopsy.

So, everything they could talk about, they actually couldn't talk about because it was hearsay. The witness who actually picked up the bullet casings from the crime scene, the witness who actually fired the recovered pistol into a vat of kinetic jelly, the forensic pathologist who sliced open the cadaver—those people had to tell the jury themselves what they did. So much worse, then, if the witness wasn't even the real lead detective, but instead was just the 'acting' lead detective. If Chen couldn't tell the jury what the ballistics guy told him, then Montero definitely couldn't tell the jury what Chen told her the ballistics guy told him.

And she hadn't even attended the autopsy.

So, Brunelle took her through the case, letting her play tour guide to what the jury would hear from later witnesses, all the while knowing the real tour guide had been "injured in the line of duty" and was "unavailable to testify." The only thing she could really testify about firsthand was the interrogation of the defendant, and even that would only yield one word.

That portion of her testimony was at the very end—after arriving at the scene, checking in with Chen, observing the body, noticing but not supervising the collection of evidence, surrounding the defendant's apartment complex, and taking the defendant into custody. Then she could testify about something she actually heard.

Too bad it also helped the defense.

"Once you, Detective Chen, and Mr. Nguyen were all seated in the interrogation room," Brunelle asked Montero, "did you advise him of his Constitutional rights?"

"Yes, sir," Montero confirmed. "We use a standard advisement form. We advised him of his right to remain silent and his right to an attorney."

"And after you advised him of his rights, did he agree to speak with you?"

Montero thought for a moment. "Sort of."

"Sort of?" Brunelle repeated. "What do you mean?"

"He definitely agreed to speak with us," she clarified. "But when he did, it was only two words. Or maybe one; I think it's hyphenated. But anyway, only one short phrase."

"What was that phrase?"

It was the phrase Welles told the jury meant his client was innocent.

"Self-defense," Montero answered. "That was the only thing he said, but he said it like three or four times. We asked him what happened and he said, 'self-defense.' We asked him to expand, but he just said, 'self-defense' again. We asked him a few different ways to give us details, to tell us his side of the story, but every time we did, he just answered, 'self-defense'. Eventually, we terminated the interview."

But it was also the phrase that put the gun in Nguyen's hand.

"Was it significant to you that Mr. Nguyen said, 'self-defense' when you asked him what happened?" Brunelle continued.

"Well, yeah," Montero answered.

"Why?"

"Because it meant he shot the victim," Montero turned and told the jury. "Up until that point all we had was a suspect description and a partial license plate. Tall, skinny, Asian man at one a.m. in the International District isn't going to be enough to identify the perp, you know what I mean? If he had refused to talk to us, we might not have been able to pin the shooting on him. But when he opened his mouth and said, 'self-defense,' well, we knew one thing: we had the shooter."

And that was why Brunelle had to admit Nguyen's otherwise self-serving claim of self-defense.

"Thank you, Detective Montero," Brunelle concluded. "No further questions."

Welles waited a moment to allow Brunelle to vacate the well in front of the witness stand, then stepped around his counsel table and straight up to the witness stand.

"Detective Montero," he began from his location far too close to her, "I'm going to ask you a series of yes-or-no questions. Please limit your responses to 'yes' or 'no.' If you don't believe you can answer the question with a 'yes' or a 'no,' then please tell me only that, and I will attempt to rephrase the question. Do not use that as an opportunity to offer a lengthy narrative answer to my yes-or-no question. Do you understand?"

Montero bristled a bit at being addressed so brusquely, but she gave a stiff nod. "Yes."

"Good." Welles then stepped back from the witness stand to leave a more comfortable space between himself and the witness. "Now, let's begin. You were not the original lead detective on this case, correct?"

"Correct," Montero answered. "I mean, yes."

"So, you did not have primary responsibility for, say, the recovery of evidence at the scene?"

"No, I did not," Montero admitted.

"And you did not interview scene witnesses like Mr. Han?"

"No, I did not.

"And you did not attend the autopsy, correct?"

"Correct. I did not."

"In fact, for every significant aspect of this investigation," Welles pressed, "you were not the acting lead detective, but rather merely assisting

Detective Chen."

Montero thought for several seconds before answering. "No," she said finally. "That is not true."

Brunelle fought to keep a smile off his face in front of the jury. Welles had just stepped in it. Or at least his shoe was hovering over it.

Unfortunately, Welles could see it too, and attempted to pull his foot back.

"Allow me to rephrase," he began, but Brunelle wasn't going to let the opportunity pass that easily.

"Your Honor," Brunelle stood up and interrupted, "I have a motion." Then, of course, "Outside the presence of the jury."

"That's not necessary," Welles insisted. "I withdraw the question. I will rephrase. I believe I know what Mr. Brunelle's motion is, and I assure the Court there is no need to hear it. I will move on."

"With all due respect to Mr. Welles," Brunelle responded, "I don't think he should be the one to determine whether the Court hears my motion, let alone what the Court's ruling should be. This is important, Your Honor, and related to our last motion outside the jury's presence. It may impact further examination of this witness, so we need to address it now."

Judge Tillerson sighed, a long, deep sigh. Then he nodded to his bailiff before turning again to the jury. "Ladies and gentlemen, I'm going to ask you to go into the jury room one more time while I speak with the attorneys. I realize this may be tiresome, but I assure you I would not interrupt the trial unless I felt it was necessary and appropriate to do so."

The jury box surrendered another chorus of whispers and moans, but the jurors did as they were told and followed the bailiff into the jury room. Tillerson could barely wait for the door to close before he tore into the attorneys.

"Before you say anything, Mr. Brunelle, your motion is denied. I know you're going to argue that Mr. Welles opened the door to the shooting of Detective Chen when he said she hadn't been lead during *any* portion of the case, but I don't think he did. Or rather, if he did, it was only a crack, and

I'm not going to let you try to drive a truck through that crack."

"Thank you, Your Honor," Welles piped up.

"And you." The judge pointed at Welles. "Stop dancing on the edge of the cliff. If you bump that door open so much as one more millimeter, I will not only let Mr. Brunelle drive a truck through it, I hold the door open myself while he does it. Is that understood?"

Welles was speechless, but only for a moment of course. "Y—Yes, Your Honor."

"Good," Tillerson huffed. "Now, if I recall correctly, Mr. Welles, you had withdrawn the question. So, Detective Montero, don't answer it. Mr. Welles, you can ask more questions if you want, or you can be smart, realize you've made your point, and sit down so we don't turn this courtroom into a truck stop."

He nodded to the bailiff who was waiting right next to the door to the jury room. "Bring them back in," he ordered.

The bailiff opened the door, the jurors filed back into the jury box, and the judge glowered down at the defense attorney. "Any further questions?"

Welles considered for a moment, but then smiled broadly and acquiesced. "No, Your Honor. Thank you. No further questions."

There wasn't anything to rehabilitate on really, so Brunelle elected not to attempt any redirect-examination. Montero was excused, and the judge was finished.

"We are going to recess for the day now, ladies and gentlemen," he told the jury. "We will reconvene at nine o'clock tomorrow morning to hear the testimony of the next witness for the State. Thank you and good night."

Everyone stood as first the jurors, then the judge, filed out of the courtroom. Once they were all gone and court was truly in recess, Meckle turned to Brunelle.

"Wow," he said. "Judge Tillerson sure was angry."

But Brunelle shook his head. "He wasn't angry. He was just making sure we understood him. No matter what Welles does on cross, the door is never going to be open wide enough to let us talk about what happened to

Chen."

"So, we're sunk on that, huh?"

"No," Brunelle answered. "That's what Tillerson's been trying to tell us, to tell *me*. There is a way. One way. But I may have ruined it."

"How?"

"By having Montero tell the jury what Nguyen said," Brunelle realized. "Now Welles may not put him on the stand."

CHAPTER 36

The next series of witnesses were the ones who needed to testify instead of Montero. The officers who sealed off the crime scene, the evidence technicians who recovered the casings and the gun from the parking lot, the S.W.A.T. sergeant who headed up the apprehension of the defendant. Each important, but none having direct evidence of whether or why Nguyen shot Ostrander.

Welles reverted to his short, surgical cross. Some were more effective than others. The senior evidence technician admitted that it's always possible a piece of evidence could be overlooked, especially using flashlights in the dark of the night. But the S.W.A.T. sergeant wasn't about to admit their response had been overkill. If anything, Mr. Nguyen should be grateful he was alive at all.

The last two witnesses were the most important to the State's case, in part because the State's case was completely circumstantial. Almost completely. There was direct evidence of the shooting: the only surviving witness, Nguyen himself, had admitted to shooting the victim. But what made that shooting illegal—what made it not self-defense—that was all circumstantial.

The biggest problem for Brunelle (and Meckle, he supposed) was that the victim had a gun a few inches from his hand when he was discovered.

That left two possibilities. The first, and most obvious, was that Ostrander had a gun in his hand at the time he was shot. The second, and less likely possibility, was that Nguyen planted it there after killing him. But that would have required Nguyen to have had two guns on him, because the second-to-last witness was about to tell the jury that the gun found next to Peter Ostrander did not fire the bullets that killed him.

"Please state your name for the record," Meckle began the direct examination of the State's ballistics expert.

"Harold Brackenridge," the rotund, middle aged man in the tight suit coat and short necktie answered.

"How are you employed, Mr. Brackenridge?"

"I am a forensic firearm examiner with the Washington State Patrol Crime Laboratory," was the answer.

And they were off. Meckle had the standard script everyone in the office used for whichever firearms expert the Crime Lab assigned to your case. It was pretty simple. Every gun barrel had microscopic imperfections, tiny raised bumps, that scratched the bullets that traveled down that barrel in a unique way. A fingerprint, but for a gun. And the ejector pin that spit the casings out of a semi-automatic handgun after every shot left a unique mark as well on the casing left behind. So, with a little knowledge and a decent microscope, any firearms expert could tell you, "No, the bullet extracted from Mr. Ostrander's skull, and the two casings recovered in the parking lot on the night in question were not fired from the pistol recovered from the same parking lot on the same night."

"In fact," Meckle concluded—off-script because a standard script can't cover everything, "the handgun recovered that night still had a full magazine at the time it was recovered."

Brackenridge hedged his answer just slightly. "That is how I received it, yes." But it was okay. The evidence tech who had recovered it confirmed he cleared it for storage and noted a full magazine and an empty chamber.

"Thank you, Mr. Brackenridge," Meckle finished. "I have no further questions for this witness, Your Honor."

Welles stood up and waited for Meckle to sit down before beginning his cross-examination. He elected to do it from his spot behind the defense table, gesturing at the witness with the pen in his hand.

"Full magazine does not equal full gun, correct?"

"It depends on your definition of full, I suppose," Brackenridge answered, sort of.

"There could also be a round in the chamber, correct?" Welles pressed him.

"Correct," Brackenridge admitted. "You can load a cartridge into the chamber manually in addition to the ones in the magazine."

"So, the firearm recovered that night could have fired a shot, but still have a full magazine, correct?"

Brackenridge thought for a moment. "I don't think so. When the round in the chamber fired, the actual of the weapon should have loaded a round from the magazine. If the magazine was full, that means no rounds were loaded into the chamber, which means no shot was fired."

"The round in the magazine could have jammed, correct?" Welles challenged, "Preventing it from loading properly."

Brackenridge frowned. "That's theoretically possible, but very rare. I didn't have any problems with jamming when I examined and test-fired the weapon."

"But it is possible?"

"Theoretically," Brackenridge answered.

"Theoretically possible," Welles insisted.

"Yes," Brackenridge relented.

"Also," Welles continued. "If there were a round in the chamber, and no magazine in the gun at the time of the shot—the magazine being inserted into the gun after the shot—that is another way that weapon could have fired a shot that night but still have had a full magazine."

"I suppose," Brackenridge admitted. "If the shooter had the time to do that. And the inclination. That would be a strange way to handle your firearm."

"Unless you were trying to cover something up?" Welles suggested.

"I guess," Brackenridge replied, "but there were no fired bullets or ejected casings found that matched the gun. I would expect those if the gun had actually been fired."

"Unless the fired bullet," Welles posited, "missed its intended target and flew off into the night, coming to rest somewhere law enforcement didn't know to look, correct?"

Brackenridge thought for a moment, then conceded, "Yes, that's possible."

"And unless the ejected casing," Welles continued, "was kicked clear of the crime scene by the shooter, or any number of people who could have entered that crime scene before or even after the police arrived several minutes after the shooting, correct?"

"That seems unlikely to me," Brackenridge said, "but not impossible."

"Not impossible," Welles repeated. "Thank you."

Brunelle was going to suggest to Meckle that he didn't need to redirect, but his co-counsel jumped to his feet before he could.

"Not impossible," Meckle also repeated. "But would you say it's reasonable?"

Great question, Brunelle had to admit to himself.

And Brackenridge knew what to do with it. "No, it's not reasonable."

And they only had to prove it beyond a reasonable doubt.

"No further questions," Meckle said.

Welles had no recross based on just that one question, so they were done with Brackenridge. That left one more witness. And damn everything, Brunelle was going to do the direct exam.

He stood up and announced, "The State calls Dr. Marianne Delacourt."

CHAPTER 37

"Are you sure you should be doing this examination?" Meckle whispered to Brunelle as Delacourt entered the courtroom. "You could give me your script. It's not too late."

Brunelle shook his head slightly as he watched Delacourt step up to the judge to be sworn in. "Sorry, Greg. I don't use scripts any more."

"You may proceed whenever you're ready," Judge Tillerson advised Brunelle as Delacourt sat down in the witness chair and decidedly did not smile as Brunelle approached her.

"Hello, Dr. Delacourt," he started. "Could you state your name and occupation for the record?"

Delacourt turned to deliver her answers to the jury. That was fine with Brunelle. She seemed willing to smile at them.

"Marianne Delacourt. I am an Assistant Medical Examiner with the King County Medical Examiner's Office."

"What are some of your duties as an Assistant Medical Examiner as they might relate to a criminal case like the one we're here for today?"

Delacourt sighed slightly. "Not all of my work relates to criminal cases. In fact, a very large portion of the autopsies I conduct have nothing to do with crimes at all."

"So, you conduct autopsies?" Brunelle pulled from her response.

"Yes," Delacourt replied sharply. "I conduct autopsies."

"Did you conduct an autopsy on a man named Peter Ostrander?"

"I suppose I did," Delacourt practically admitted as she pulled open the file she had brought with her to the witness stand, "or else you wouldn't have me here now." She put on a pair of reading glasses and perused the file. "Yes," she confirmed. "I did conduct an autopsy on a Peter Michael Ostrander, white male, twenty-three years old. Multiple gunshot wounds."

Brunelle refrained from saying, 'That's him!'

"Did you also respond to the scene and collect Mr. Ostrander's body?" he asked instead.

"Oh, yes," Delacourt sneered. "I recall you were there as well. I recall that very clearly."

Brunelle, who was standing a little farther away than he usually did when direct-examining his own witnesses, pressed on.

"When was the autopsy conducted in relation to the shooting?" he asked.

"The very next morning," Delacourt told the jury. "The body was kept in refrigeration until we were able to get to it."

"Is that normal procedure?" Brunelle wanted the jury to know.

"Obviously, it is," Delacourt sniped. "We have refrigeration units precisely for that function. We don't put the bodies in the kitchen refrigerator."

Lovely, Brunelle thought, but kept his poker face. And anyway, a couple of the jurors laughed slightly, so that meant they liked her. Which was a good thing. Probably.

"Could you tell the jury what you're looking for when you conduct an autopsy?" Brunelle continued.

"I am looking for the manner and cause of death," Delacourt explained. "Manner of death means one of four possible categories: homicide, suicide, accident, or natural causes. Cause of death speaks the exact mechanism of death, for example, sharp force trauma or a gunshot wound."

"Thank you," Brunelle felt compelled to say. "Were you able to determine a cause of death in this case?"

Delacourt paused long enough to give him a 'did you really just ask that?' expression. "Um, yes. There were two gunshot wounds. One to the torso which perforated a lung, and a second which penetrated his skull. The gunshot to the torso was potentially fatal without medical intervention, but the gunshot wound to the head was instantly fatal."

"And were you able to determine a manner of death?" Brunelle continued.

Delacourt nodded and turned to the jury. "The manner of death was homicide."

"How did you determine that?" Brunelle followed up.

"Well, a gunshot wound isn't always homicide," Delacourt explained. "It could also be suicide or accident. In this case, however, there was no evidence that the gunshot wound was self-inflicted. In addition, the police had arrested a subject who had, I was told, admitted to shooting the decedent, so it didn't; appear to be an accident either."

"So, you rely on eyewitness reports and other outside evidence when determining the manner of death?"

"I prefer not to," Delacourt answered, "but sometimes it's unavoidable. When I go to a crime scene and there's a dead body and the police are actively seeking the shooter, I know that. When I go to a home and the family is crying about the gun going off accidentally, I know that too. But I believe those sorts of things are confirmed, more reliably, from things like distance of the shot, angle of entry, trajectories."

"Were those sorts of things helpful to you in this case?"

Delacourt answered, "Yes," even as Welles stood up and called out, "Objection! There's no argument that this wasn't a homicide. The issue is whether it was a murder. That's a legal issue and one on which this witness is neither qualified nor, I'm certain, willing to render an opinion."

"I understand your objection," Judge Tillerson said without even giving Brunelle a chance to respond, "and it is overruled. You may answer the question, doctor."

"I'll repeat the question," Brunelle offered.

But Delacourt interrupted him. "No need, counselor. I'm capable of remembering a question asked of me ten seconds ago. You asked if there were any findings from my autopsy which supported a conclusion of homicide over suicide or accident."

Brunelle nodded. That was pretty much what he'd asked, although not in so many words.

"The answer, as I already stated, is yes," Delacourt continued.

"And what were those findings, exactly?"

"Objection!" Welles interrupted again. "Calls for a narrative answer."

All questions call for a narrative answer, Brunelle thought ruefully

"Can you ask a more specific question?" Judge Tillerson requested.

"Yes, Your Honor," Brunelle agreed. He turned back to Delacourt. "Were there any findings regarding the distance of the shots?"

"Yes," Delacourt answered. "When a bullet exits the barrel of a gun, there are trace amounts of unburnt gunpowder and even flame which follow behind the bullet. These dissipate after about eighteen inches. So, if there were no burns from the muzzle or stippling from the gunpowder, then I can, and in this case did, conclude that the shots occurred at a distance greater than eighteen inches. I can't say how much more than eighteen inches, but it was more."

Brunelle nodded. That was useful, and relatively painless to extract from her. "What about the sites or trajectories of the gunshot wounds? Were there any findings there that contributed to your conclusion that this was a homicide?"

Delacourt thought for several seconds. Finally, she answered, "No."

"No?" Brunelle parroted instinctively. "Are you sure?"

"Oh, yes." Delacourt finally smiled at him. "I'm sure. The angles and trajectories I'm speaking of are in relation to the body itself, not anything outside of it. I can tell you, for example, that the shot to the head entered at an angle of approximately ninety degrees in relation to the main head-to-toe line of the body. What I can't tell you is whether he was standing up, squatting, or lying down when that occurred. He could have been standing up with the shooter pointing the gun parallel to the ground, or he could have been lying on his back, with the gun perpendicular to the ground. There's no way for me, or anyone, to know."

"Unless they saw it," Brunelle was quick to point out.

"Did someone see it?" she asked back.

Brunelle frowned slightly and ignored the question. "Was the bullet which entered the torso recovered at autopsy?"

"No, that was a through-and-through shot," Delacourt explained. "The bullet exited the subject's back. It flew off into the night never to be recovered for all I know."

Great, Brunelle thought sarcastically. *Just like the shot Peter Ostrander fired before inserting the magazine in his gun.*

"What about the bullet that entered the head?" Brunelle soldiered on. "Was that recovered at autopsy?"

"Yes, that one was recovered from inside his skull," Delacourt answered. "Skulls are very thick, and bullets lose a lot of velocity when they penetrate the bone. They usually don't have enough energy left to exit through the skull again, so instead they ricochet and tear through the brain tissue."

"Is that what happened here?"

"Yes, that's what happened here."

Brunelle took some solace in knowing that he was almost done. "Did you check the hands for gunshot residue?"

Delacourt sighed again and actually rolled her eyes a bit. "Yes, but only a preliminary screening test."

"Why did you administer the test?"

"Because the detective asked me to," Delacourt answered. "It's not actually relevant to my findings."

Brunelle ignored the editorial comment at the end of her response. "What was the result of that preliminary screening test for gunshot residue?"

"It was negative," Delacourt admitted.

"So, to summarize," Brunelle was ready to sit down, "Peter Ostrander was shot twice, from a distance greater than eighteen inches, the shot to the head was instantly fatal and could have been delivered while he was lying down, and he never fired a gun that night. Is that all correct?"

Delacourt thought for a moment then answered. "The manner of death was homicide, and the cause of death was a gunshot wound to the head. All that stuff you just said is consistent with my findings, but I can't say that's what happened."

Brunelle finally smiled himself. "That's okay," he said. "I will."

He was almost done. In fact, he didn't really have any more questions for her. But he needed to set up something for later in the trial. Something he might need, depending on what Welles did when it was his turn to put on a case-in-chief. Which meant he didn't want Welles to know he was doing it. He walked over to the bailiff and collected up several clear baggies that had been sealed with evidence tape and marked as exhibits.

"Doctor," he began as he returned to his spot in front of the witness stand, "I'm going to hand you several items, marked Exhibits Thirty-Four through Thirty-Seven. Could you just check those and confirm they were recovered from the victim at his autopsy?"

"I can confirm that right now," Delacourt sniped. "The baggies all have my autopsy report number on them, as well as Mr. Ostrander's name, the date of the autopsy, and Detective Chen's signature over the evidence tape after he sealed them in my presence."

Perfect, Brunelle thought. "Oh, okay. I guess that will do," he said. "Thank you." Then he looked up to the judge and announced, "No further questions."

Welles shot out from behind his counsel table, ready to use the good doctor to drive home his main point. "Homicide does not necessarily equal murder, does it?"

"No, not at all," Delacourt agreed. She seemed happy to agree, in fact. "All murders are homicides but not all homicides are murders."

"You can say this was a homicide," Welles went on, "but you can't say whether this was a murder, can you?"

"I cannot," Delacourt answered, "and I would not."

"And even if Mr. Ostrander never fired his gun," Welles put to her, "if he so much as displayed it in a threatening manner, it would have been reasonable and appropriate for Mr. Nguyen to use lawful force to defend himself, wouldn't you agree?"

But before she could, Brunelle stood up. "Objection, Your Honor. That calls for a legal conclusion."

"It certainly does," Welles agreed, with a knowing look to the jurors.

"Objection sustained," Tillerson ruled. "Any further questions, Mr. Welles?"

"No, Your Honor, nothing further," Welles answered. But then he raised a hand. "Oh, wait. I do have one more question for the good doctor." He turned and grinned at her. "Why didn't you want to work with Mr. Brunelle?"

"Objection!" Brunelle called out again. Then, grasping for a reason other than having to explain that stupid joke one more time. "Eh, relevance."

Tillerson should have sustained the objection, but instead he told Delacourt, "You may answer if you're able."

Delacourt looked at Brunelle, then up at the judge. "He has a lousy sense of humor."

CHAPTER 38

Delacourt was the last witness for the State. After she stepped down from the witness stand, Brunelle stood to declare, "The State rests."

Tillerson then inquired of Welles whether he intended to put on a case. But of course he did. He told the jury as much in opening. His only request was that they start fresh the next morning, so he could have time to digest the totality of the State's case before calling his client to the stand. It was a standard request and Tillerson granted it without objection from the State.

So, the next morning, bright and early at the usual 9:00 a.m. start time, court was reconvened. The courtroom was packed. It was a big deal when the defendant testified, especially on a murder case. First of all, not every defendant testified. Second, if he testified, it meant he would be cross-examined, and a defendant being cross-examined by the prosecutor was about as intense as a criminal trial could get. There was no equivalent on the other side. A defense attorney cross examining the lead detective was about as close as it got, and really, it wasn't even close. The lead detective was still just a witness, not a party. And in this case, he didn't testify at all.

Carlisle had gotten herself a literal front row seat in the gallery. There were others from the Prosecutor's Office, including Nicole who'd found a seat in the back. There were defense attorneys too, including Jessica Edwards from the Public Defender's Office and several members of the private defense bar. A few cops were sprinkled in there, along with reporters, general spectators, and, of course, the family. They'd all come to see what story the defendant would tell. And how the prosecutor would tear it apart.

Brunelle felt bad that he was likely to disappoint them.

Judge Tillerson took the bench promptly at 9:00 a.m., which he was wont to do. The jury was brought in. Then Welles stood up and announced, "The defense calls Jeremy Nguyen to the stand."

Nguyen stood up and walked forward to be sworn in. He was still being held in custody, but the jury wasn't supposed to know that, so he was dressed in street clothes—a dress shirt and nice pants, no tie—and the uniformed corrections officers pretended like they were just standard security. Except that, in anticipation of Nguyen moving from the defense table to the witness stand, one of the two officers had taken up a station near the door to the jury room, because it had its own door to the hallway, and freedom beyond.

"Could you please state your full name for the record?" Welles began.

"Jeremy Huy Nguyen," his client answered. He seemed relaxed enough, given the circumstances. Not exactly confident, but not scared either. Prepared. And that made sense. There was no way Welles was going to put a client on the stand without making sure they both knew exactly what bullshit they were going to try to sell to the jury.

Welles started with personal background; the stuff they taught at the defense seminars was supposed to humanize the client. Nguyen was born and raised in Seattle. His grandparents were immigrants from Vietnam. He lived right outside the International District and took the bus to his job as a cook at one of the many restaurants there. The money was good enough, especially with no family to support yet, but he was hoping to meet a special girl and settle down, have kids, get his slice of the American Dream.

Puke. Brunelle hoped the jury wasn't buying it, but a quick glance over at them only revealed they were all paying close attention to Nguyen's testimony.

"I'd like to turn our attention to the night in question," Welles said. "Do you recall the events of the night you were arrested?"

Nguyen nodded. "I sure do."

"What were you doing that night?"

"I was working a late shift at the restaurant," Nguyen explained, "but my manager told me I could go home early. That meant I could leave at one instead of two. It was a nice night, so I was just going to walk home."

"Did you make it home that night?"

"I did eventually," Nguyen answered. "But something happened first. Something terrible."

Double puke.

"What happened, Jeremy?" Welles's voice dripped with concern.

"I was cutting through the parking lot at Eighth and Jackson, the one that's underneath I-5," Nguyen said, "when some guy started yelling something at me. I tried to ignore him at first, but he kept yelling and started walking toward me, so I stopped to see who he was. You know, like maybe I knew him or something? And to see what his problem was."

"Did you know him?"

"No, I'd never seen him before in my life," Nguyen said.

"What did he look like?" Welles asked.

Nguyen shrugged. "He was like my age. White. He looked bigger than me. And he looked really angry."

"What was he angry about?"

"I don't know," Nguyen answered. "I was just cutting through the parking lot. I thought maybe he was homeless and thought I was trespassing on his sleeping spot or something, but really, I don't know. I was just trying to walk home."

"What happened next, Jeremy?"

Nguyen nodded for a moment, looking as if he needed a moment to steel himself against the memory. Or remember his line, Brunelle thought. "All of a sudden he ran up to me and cut off my path. He yelled something about being sick of my kind running the city. I told him I didn't want any trouble, but he just kept yelling. I thought he was drunk or high or something. I just wanted to get out of there. And then—"

"Then what, Jeremy?" Welles jumped in.

"Then he pulled out a gun."

Brunelle looked over again at the jury box to gauge reaction. No one gasped or covered their mouths in shock, so that was good. They all seemed to be just listening intently, doing their jobs. Brunelle supposed that was good too, although he wouldn't have minded seeing a juror or two with arms crossed and eyes to the ceiling.

"What did you do when he pulled out the gun?" Welles continued.

"I started backing up, with my hands raised. I told him I wasn't looking for any trouble and I could just walk home a different way."

"Did that calm him down?"

"No. If anything it made him madder. He pointed the gun right at me. I was scared he was going to shoot me. So I pulled out my own gun, but just to show him I was armed too."

"So," Welles tried to sound casual, "you also carry a gun?"

"Yes," Nguyen answered.

"Why?"

"For protection," Nguyen claimed. "I often walk home in the dark after work, so I want to feel safe."

"Well, that makes sense," Welles approved of his own client's claim. "What happened next?"

"Well, next," Nguyen hesitated, but Brunelle couldn't tell if he was doing it on purpose to seem disturbed by the memory, or he wasn't quite sure what he was supposed to say next. "Next he fired at me. Just one shot. And I guess he missed. I saw him reach into his pocket and pull out a magazine. He started pushing it into the handle of the gun. I was so scared he was going to start shooting again, I guess I just kinda shot back first."

"Of course," Welles continued to validate his client's actions. "How many shots did you fire?"

"I don't know," Nguyen claimed. "Two, I guess. I'm not a hundred percent sure. It happened so quickly. And I was so scared."

And triple puke. Brunelle shook his head slightly, hoping the jurors were doing the same thing in their minds.

"What happened next?" Welles asked. "Did you call the police?"

Nguyen shook his head. "No. I just panicked, I guess. I ran away. I didn't know if I hit him or not. I just wanted to get away. The next thing I know, the police have my apartment building surrounded."

"They wanted you to surrender yourself?" Welles asked.

"Yes."

"And did you?" Welles followed up. "Without incident?"

"Yes. I walked outside with my hands up and they arrested me."

"Did you tell them what happened?"

"I tried to," Nguyen said. "But no one wanted to listen. They just pushed me to the ground, handcuffed me, and threw me in the back of a cop car. There were a lot of them, and they were really strong. So I didn't really get a chance to say anything right then."

"What about later?" Welles followed up. "When you spoke with detectives?"

"Yeah, I told them it was self-defense," Nguyen said. "But they told me they didn't believe me, so I decided I better not say anything more until I spoke with an attorney."

Welles took a moment to nod and look thoughtful. "Is there anything else the jury should know, Jeremy?"

Nguyen nodded too. "Yes." He turned to the jury box. "I'm really sorry for what happened that night. I didn't want to shoot anyone, and I didn't mean to kill anyone. I was just really scared and I was trying to defend myself."

"Thank you, Jeremy," Welles concluded his direct-exam. "No further questions, Your Honor."

And finally it was Brunelle's turn.

Television and movies were filled with scenes where the prosecutor browbeats the defendant into admitting he lied and in fact he really did commit the crime. In reality, that never happened. Ever. Defendants knew they would be challenged on that, and they were always prepared to say, 'No, I didn't do it.' If you can't say that, you better not get on the stand. So, Brunelle knew that approach was a waste of time, even if everyone in the room, from Carlisle to Edwards to Nguyen himself expected it. So, instead of demanding Nguyen admit his lies, he asked him to confirm them.

"You walked home from work that night?"

Nguyen was cautious. "Yes." It almost sounded like a question.

"You always carry a gun on your person when you work the late shift?"

Another cautious, "Yes."

"You had never met the man under the overpass before that night?"

"No."

"No friends in common?"

"No, sir."

"Didn't know him from work? No business arrangements?"

"No, sir."

Brunelle nodded thoughtfully. "He pulled out his gun first?"

"Yes, sir."

"He shot first?"

"Yes."

"Then he loaded a magazine into his gun?"

"Yes."

"And only then did you fire your gun?"

"Absolutely."

Brunelle knew those were all lies. He didn't walk home; Timothy Han saw him drive away. He didn't carry a gun on him when he worked; he carried it on him when he went to confront a rival drug dealer. He hadn't met Ostrander for the first time that night; he knew him at least well enough to know he was competition for Joaninha's business. Ostrander never shot his gun; Han only heard two shots and there were two holes in Ostrander's body. And he didn't watch patiently while Ostrander loaded a magazine into his gun to explain Welles's crazy theory about how a fully loaded gun could still have fired a round.

He could point those all out in closing, in case some of the jurors hadn't already noticed the inconsistencies.

But there was one lie that mattered the most. The one that opened the door to what really happened that night.

"So," Brunelle looked Nguyen straight in the eye, "it was self-defense?"

Nguyen nodded strongly. "Yes. It was self-defense."

Brunelle held his gaze for a moment longer, then looked up at the judge and raised a hand. "No further questions, Your Honor." And he strode back to the prosecution table.

Welles stood up, seemingly surprised by the brief, and confirmatory, cross-examination. "No redirect-examination, Your Honor." Which meant his client could get off the stand while his lies were still warm.

Brunelle stood behind his counsel table, motionless, his eyes following Nguyen as he made his way from the witness stand back to his seat at the defense table. The corrections officers watched him too, but for different reasons, just in case he might make a run for it. But after Brunelle's minimalist cross-exam, Nguyen looked pretty confident. Cocky, even.

"I thought you'd be tougher on him," Meckle whispered. "Not that you did anything wrong. I mean, I just thought…" he let his words trail off.

Brunelle turned around to the gallery to confirm Meckle's sentiment was shared. It was. Carlisle looked him dead in the eye and mouthed, 'What the fuck was that?'

But Brunelle didn't care. He only had one audience that mattered. He just needed Welles to say those three magic words so he could address that audience.

"We have no further witnesses, Your Honor," Welles announced. "The defense rests."

Yeah, those three words.

Brunelle's audience looked down at him from the bench, his

expression inscrutable. But Brunelle thought he could scrute it anyway. "Does the State wish to put on any rebuttal evidence, Mr. Brunelle?"

It was a standard question, usually met with a standard reply of 'No.' Rebuttal evidence was rare in a criminal case—not unheard of, but rare. The reason was that rebuttal was designed to respond to the defense's case-in-chief, but in a criminal case the prosecution usually let it all hang out in their own case-in-chief, which came prior to the defense case. The other reason it was rare was that, often, the defense didn't put on any evidence at all. Defendants exercised their rights not to testify, and there weren't any other witnesses to call. That was because most defendants were guilty as hell and didn't have any witnesses to say otherwise. Still, the judge always asked it.

And Brunelle answered it. "Yes, Your Honor." Followed by the prudent suggestion, punctuated my Welles jumping to his feet at Brunelle's 'Yes,' that, "Perhaps we should discuss this outside the presence of the jury."

"Rebuttal?" Welles interrupted. "Your Honor, if Mr. Brunelle is suggesting what I think he's suggesting, I think the Court can go ahead and deny that out of hand, without the need of a lengthy hearing outside the presence of the jury."

Tillerson nodded thoughtfully at Welles. Then he turned to his bailiff. "Take the jury out."

The bailiff jumped up and hurried across the courtroom to lead the jurors to the jury room. They didn't murmur this time. They filed wordlessly into the jury room as the judge and the lawyers waited for the click of the door to signal they could speak freely.

"Go ahead, Mr. Brunelle," Judge Tillerson said once the door closed.

"Could I be heard first, Your Honor?" Welles interrupted.

"No," Tillerson answered. Turned away again. "Go on, Mr. Brunelle."

"Thank you, Your Honor." He took another moment to glance quickly around the courtroom. Carlisle was wearing a very slight, very crooked smile that showed she thought he might actually know what he was doing. "Your Honor, I would ask the Court to revisit its earlier ruling suppressing the evidence obtained shortly before trial, namely the identity of the person known as Joaninha, the shooting of Detective Chen, and the resultant confession by Joaninha that she had been in contact with both the defendant and the victim about possible drug transactions, thereby establishing a motive for the murder."

Welles released a bark of a laugh. "That is preposterous, Your Honor. The Court was correct to suppress the evidence at the beginning of trial and nothing has changed since the Court's ruling that would justify allowing the evidence in now—certainly not the testimony of my client explaining how he defended himself. He never once mentioned this Joe-oh-nina person. Mr. Brunelle is desperate and grasping for any rope in the coming maelstrom of his defeat."

"Actually, Your Honor," Brunelle put in, "I misspoke when I asked the Court to reconsider its earlier ruling. Your earlier ruling was that this evidence was not admissible in the State's case-in-chief. I'm not asking to present it in my case-in-chief, obviously. That's already over. But I am asking to present it now, in rebuttal, to answer the defendant's testimony and allow the jury the opportunity to weigh the defendant's testimony accordingly."

"Your Honor," Welles complained. "This is ridiculous. It would be laughable, really, if it weren't so serious. There was a reason the Court excluded this evidence at the beginning of trial, and that reason went to the right of my client to a fair and speedy trial. Those rights have not changed. And I am no more prepared to respond to these spurious and specious allegations than I was when we began this trial."

Tillerson nodded once and then pointed down at Welles. "Let me ask you this, Mr. Welles. Let's say your client had made a longer, fuller statement to the police. Let's say it was fairly detailed and was an admission to the crime charged. But let's also say that the police failed to read your client his Constitutional rights before interrogating him. Would that confession be admissible in the State's case-in-chief?"

"I see where you're going with this," Welles began with a dismissive wave of his hand, "but I hardly think—"

"Would that confession," Judge Tillerson interrupted him, "be admissible in the State's case-in-chief?"

Welles exhaled audibly. "No, Your Honor. I would hope it would not be."

"Correct," Tillerson replied. "It would not be. Now, suppose the defendant in such a case took the stand, after the State rested its case-in-chief, and told a story very different from what he told the police that night. Perhaps an alibi. He was up all night with his sick grandmother. Wouldn't the State then be allowed to use his prior statement to impeach his current testimony?"

"Again, Your Honor," Welles protested, "this is entirely—"

"Wouldn't the State," Tillerson repeated the question, his voice raised, "be allowed to use his prior statement to challenge his in-court testimony?"

Welles just stood there, his fists clenched. He didn't have an answer for the judge.

But that was okay, because the judge already knew the answer. "Yes, they would. The case law is crystal clear on that. A defendant cannot use the suppression of illegally obtained evidence from the State's case-in-chief as a blank check to lie to the jury with impunity."

"My client was not lying," Welles insisted, his own voice raised.

Judge Tillerson shrugged. "Maybe he wasn't. Maybe he was. That's not for me to say. But you put him on the stand and had him tell the jury himself that it was self-defense, even knowing what evidence Mr. Brunelle wanted to put on. You knew the risk in that. I think you just hoped Mr. Brunelle didn't. So, you gambled, but you lost. I'm going to admit the evidence."

Meckle stood up and slapped Brunelle on the back. But the celebration was short-lived. Or at least was quickly tempered.

"But Mr. Brunelle," the judge continued, "the evidence rules still apply, and so does the Confrontation Clause. It won't be sufficient to just put Detective Montero on the stand and ask her to tell the jury what everyone else told her. Are you still able to put on a rebuttal case?"

Brunelle offered a slight shrug and a modest grin. "I will do my best,

Your Honor."

"Will you be ready to start first thing in the morning?" Tillerson inquired.

Brunelle considered for a moment. He knew who he needed to gather as witnesses, and he was pretty sure he knew where to find them. "Yes, Your Honor."

But he was going to need some help.

Judge Tillerson ended the court day at that point, cutting off any further argument from Welles and instructing the bailiff to excuse the jurors for the day directly from the jury room. Once the room was cleared of judge and jury, the corrections officers prepared Nguyen for transport back to the jail, and Brunelle turned to a trusted partner for help.

"You available to serve some subpoenas tonight?" he asked Carlisle.

She smiled broadly. "Fuck, yeah."

CHAPTER 39

"So, what's the plan?" Carlisle asked as they drove to their destination.

"I was thinking you hand the subpoena to the witness," Brunelle deadpanned from the driver's seat, "and then the witness comes to court. That's how subpoenas work, right?"

"Not that, you jerk," Carlisle laughed. "I know how subpoenas work. No, I mean tomorrow. What's the plan for your rebuttal case? Tillerson made it pretty clear Montero won't be able to tell the jury what Oliveira told her. You gonna try to put Oliveira on the stand? She's looking at attempted murder of a cop. No way her lawyer lets her testify. Not unless you give her immunity. Oh my God, you're not going to give her immunity, are you?"

"Give immunity to someone who shot a cop?" Brunelle asked rhetorically. "Who shot my best friend? No, of course not."

Carlisle tipped her head at him. "Your best friend? Aw, that's nice."

"And you can shut up now," Brunelle said.

"Because I hurt your feelings?" Carlisle asked in a singsong voice.

"No, because we're here."

Carlisle looked out the window. "Where's here?"

"Seattle Capoeira Alliance," Brunelle answered. "Home, I hope, of our first witness."

"That chick from the pool hall?" Carlisle responded. "Oh, Davey, you two hit it off. That's nice too."

Brunelle turned off the engine and looked at the studio, a class visible through the picture window. "Yeah, that's not exactly how it turned out."

* * *

"Well, if it isn't Narc and Narckette," Abbie practically shouted when she saw them enter the studio, interrupting the session. "To what do I owe this displeasure?"

"Hi, Abbie," Brunelle said. "Do you have a minute?"

"No, actually," Abbie answered. She grabbed a towel and water bottle off the floor. She wiped the back of her neck and took a long drink. "I'm in the middle of a workout right now."

"Oh, that's okay," Carlisle responded. She waited for Abbie to finish her drink, then handed her the subpoena. "We don't need you until tomorrow morning. Nine a.m. sharp. Wear something nice."

Abbie looked down at the subpoena in her hand. "Are you fucking kidding me? I told you I didn't want to get involved, and now I have to fucking testify?"

"Sorry," Brunelle said.

"Not sorry," Carlisle added. "But justice must prevail, or something."

Abbie ran a hand through her thick, sweaty hair. "I really don't want to do this, Dave. I caused enough trouble. Joaninha, your friend… I just don't want to be involved any more."

"Look, it's not that big of a deal," Brunelle tried to reassure her. "I just need someone who can tell the jury who Joaninha is. That's it. But the judge said it has to come from you, not a cop who learned it from you. Or worse, learned it from me after I learned it from you. That's like triple hearsay or something."

He put a hand on her shoulder. "Please. It'll only take a few minutes, but it's hugely important to our case."

Abbie looked at his hand on her shoulder. Then she grabbed it by the wrist and twisted Brunelle against the wall. "I don't give a shit about your case," she growled over his shoulder.

"But you don't want us to have you arrested for ignoring a subpoena," Carlisle chimed in, making absolutely no effort to rescue Brunelle.

Abbie grunted in frustration, then gave Brunelle another shove into the wall as she released her grip on his arm. "Fuck you, Narckette. And fuck you, too, Dave."

"Delightful," Carlisle said. "See you tomorrow then. M'kay. Bye now."

Brunelle didn't say anything further; he just followed Carlisle toward the exit.

"I like her," Carlisle remarked as they reached the car. "She's spunky."

"Yeah," Brunelle agreed.

"And you really, really suck at dating," Carlisle laughed.

Brunelle laughed a little, too, despite himself. "Yeah."

* * *

The next stop was going to be both easier and harder. Easier, because the target of the subpoena wasn't likely to smash Brunelle against a wall with a slick martial art move. Harder, because he wasn't likely to be able to do much of anything, and Brunelle really didn't want to see that.

"Larry," Brunelle said softly as they entered Chen's hospital room. "Are you awake?"

Chen opened his eyes slowly. He actually looked a lot better than last time Brunelle had seen him. But he still seemed tired. "Oh, hey, Dave. Hey, Gwen. Thanks for coming. What brings you guys here?"

Carlisle started to say "Subpoena," but Brunelle cut her off.

"Just wanted to visit a friend in the hospital," he said. "How are you feeling?"

"Docs say I'm doing a lot better," Chen answered. "I gotta take it easy still or I might start bleeding again."

"So, no chasing down bad guys or testifying in court any time soon, huh?" Brunelle observed.

"Afraid not," Chen confirmed. "I'm gonna be on light duty for a while, I think."

"You're gonna be on no duty for a while, I think," Brunelle countered.

Carlisle folded up the subpoena and slipped it inside her jacket pocket. "Well, everyone at the Prosecutor's Office is pulling for you. Speedy recovery and all that."

"Thanks, Gwen." Chen coughed a little as he said it.

He turned to Brunelle. "How's the trial going? I wish I could be there."

Brunelle smiled slightly. "Yeah, so do I. But it's more important you get better. You won't do me any good bleeding on the witness stand."

"Yeah, that's just gross," Carlisle piped in.

Chen laughed slightly, which turned into more coughing.

"We should probably go," Brunelle offered. "We just wanted to stop by on our way to, uh—"

"The bar," Carlisle finished. "We're headed to a bar. Nothing better to do the night before you wrap up a big murder case than get shit-faced."

"You're almost done then?" Chen asked.

"Yep," Brunelle confirmed. "Just one or two more witnesses."

"Go get 'em, Dave." Chen pumped a weak fist at his friend. "I know you can do it."

Brunelle smiled. "Thanks, Larry. I'll do my best."

* * *

"So, what the fuck are you going to do?" Carlisle asked Brunelle once they were out in the hallway and out of Chen's earshot.

"I guess I'll have to rely on Montero," Brunelle supposed. "She was there when he was shot, so she can testify about it. If I put her on the stand for that, maybe Welles will step in it and open the door to what Oliveira said."

"He stepped in it once," Carlisle said. "He won't do it a second time."

Brunelle frowned. "I know."

CHAPTER 40

9:00 a.m. the next morning came quickly, even through a worried and sleepless night.

Brunelle wasn't sure exactly how he was going to piece together his rebuttal case. Abbie would identify Maria Oliveira as Joaninha—the name from the dead man's pocket, and Montero would tell them how when they contacted Oliveira, she opened fire on them. Then he'd just have to argue the inference that Nguyen was up to no good. Although he had to admit, it made it sound a lot more like Ostrander was the one involved in something shady. And dangerous. The sort of thing you might have to defend yourself against using lawful, acquittable force.

And there was always the chance Welles might do something to open the door to Oliveira's statements. But Brunelle knew better than to rely on that. Judge Tillerson's comment about the Confrontation Clause still applying seemed to be aimed directly at any effort to introduce Oliveira's statements without actually putting her on the stand. And the only way to put her on the stand would be to give her immunity for shooting Chen. Which was not going to happen.

So, when 9:00 a.m. arrived, Brunelle was in the courtroom, ready to do his best and almost as curious as the jury and spectators to see how it would all play out. The good news was that he could start slowly. Abbie was in the hallway ready to tell the jury that Joaninha was actually Maria Oliveira. Montero was out there too, ready to tell the jury what she did to Chen. And then…. Well, he'd figure that out when he got to it.

Judge Tillerson took the bench right at 9:00 and the jurors were brought out promptly to see what evidence, if any, the State would put on to rebut the defendant's testimony.

Brunelle stood up to announce his first witness. "The State calls Abbie Bishop."

Meckle was there too, but he was done directing witnesses. His job was to take notes and look confident. And to fetch Abbie from the hallway.

She entered and immediately lit up the room. At least that's how it felt to Brunelle. She wore a royal blue suit that hid most of her tattoos and her thick curls bounced slightly as she approached the witness stand to be sworn in. Brunelle had promised her it would only take a few minutes, but given that he knew he was unlikely to ever get to see her again, he was tempted to drag out the examination. It was a temptation he could resist, but it was there nonetheless.

"Good morning," he began after she took the oath and sat down in the witness chair. "Could you please state your name for the record?"

"My name is Abbie Bishop." She answered directly to Brunelle. She didn't know to turn to the jury to deliver her answers, like they taught the cops at the academy.

"Ms. Bishop, are you familiar at all with Seattle's International District?" Brunelle asked.

"Yes, I am."

"How are you familiar with it?" Brunelle followed up.

He probably should have warned her that he would have to ask strange, open-ended questions lest he be accused of leading the witness. He had to ask his questions that way, but he kind of sounded like an idiot doing it.

"How am I familiar with it?" Abbie repeated the question back. "Well, I live and work there for starters."

"Okay," Brunelle said, as if he didn't already know that. Although he supposed he hadn't known she lived there too. He hadn't gotten that far. "And are you familiar with the Seattle Capoeira Alliance?"

"That's where I work," Abbie answered. She seemed irritated by questions Brunelle should know the answers to. "I'm a capoeira instructor there."

"Okay," Brunelle said again. It was a sort of verbal marker. It both acknowledged the answer and indicated another question was on its way. "Could you please tell the jury what capoeira is?"

Abbie looked uncertainly at the jurors, but then turned and addressed them directly. "Uh, capoeira is a martial art from Brazil. It combines traditional African fighting skills with dance and music. It's beautiful and unique, and for those of us who practice it, the capoeira community is like family."

"You said it originates from Brazil," Brunelle proceeded. "Is the Seattle Capoeira Alliance affiliated in any way with anyone in Brazil?"

"Our mestre is in Brazil," Abbie turned back to answer Brunelle directly. It was more normal to answer the person who was asking the questions. "Mestre Águia, which means 'eagle.'"

"So, your leader is in Brazil and has a Brazilian nickname?" Brunelle tried to confirm.

Abbie just looked at him, then shook her head a little. "Portuguese. It's a Portuguese nickname. They speak Portuguese in Brazil. There's no such language as Brazilian."

"Right." Brunelle nodded at her answer. "I think I knew that. Does everyone have a Portuguese nickname?"

"Pretty much. It's given to you when you earn your first cord. It's like a belt in karate, but we call it a cord."

"Okay," Brunelle said again. "What's your Portuguese capoeira nickname?"

"Boto," Abbie answered. "It's a pink river dolphin from the Amazon."

Brunelle nodded. "That sounds cool. And your master's nickname means eagle. What about your master's wife? Does she do capoeira and does she have a nickname?"

Abbie frowned slightly, but nodded. "Yes. Her real name is Maria, but her capoeira name is Joaninha."

"Joaninha," Brunelle repeated. "What does that mean?"

"It means ladybug."

"How do you spell it?" Brunelle asked. "I don't speak Portuguese."

"J-O-A—" Abbie started.

"You know what?" Brunelle interrupted. "Why don't we have you step down from the witness stand and write it out for the jury to see."

There was a large easel tucked behind and to one side of the witness stand supporting a large flip-board of paper. Brunelle pointed to it and handed Abbie a marker.

Abbie stepped down and spelled it out on the board in all caps. "J-O-A-N-I-N-H-A," she said aloud as she wrote out the letters. "Joaninha."

Brunelle nodded and smiled. He was almost done. "You can sit down again, Ms. Bishop." He walked over to the exhibits again and extracted Exhibit Thirty-Seven. Then he walked back and handed it to her. "I'm handing you what's been marked Exhibit Thirty-Seven, which has already been identified by the Assistant Medical Examiner as something that was recovered from the victim's body during the autopsy. Could you please tell us what it is and what is written on it?"

"I'm afraid I have to object at this point, Your Honor," Welles stood up to interject. "The Medical Examiner may have identified this exhibit as being recovered at autopsy, or she may not have. I recall her looking at several items at once. But in any case, it was never admitted into evidence, Your Honor."

"That's because it wasn't relevant until now, Your Honor," Brunelle countered. "But it's not at all uncommon to have one witness identify an exhibit, then admit it later through another witness once its full relevance has been established."

Brunelle was right about that last part. That was how it was done. Judge Tillerson knew it. And so did Welles.

"The objection is overruled," Tillerson announced. "You may answer."

"I'm sorry," Abbie said. "What was the question again?"

"Could you read what's on that piece of paper?" Brunelle said.

Abbie looked down at it for a moment, then back up. "It says 'Joaninha' on it," she told the jurors. "And the start of a phone number, but just the area code: '206'."

"Joaninha," Brunelle repeated. "Exactly as it's spelled up there?" he double checked, pointing to where Abbie had just written the word.

"Yes, exactly," she confirmed.

"Was Maria Oliveira—Joaninha—in town recently?" Brunelle asked. "Say, around the time of the murder in this case?"

"Yes," Abbie answered. "She came up for our annual batizado. It's kind of an annual graduation ceremony, skills expo, and party. The mestre came for it, so she did too."

"And how do you know that she came up for it?"

"Because I know her," Abbie answered. "And I saw her. And I spoke with her."

And I'm done, Brunelle thought. But before he could announce his 'No more questions' Abbie had something to add.

"Just like I saw *him*." She pointed at the defense table. "And spoke with him."

Brunelle took a beat. "Mr. Welles?" he assumed, wondering when Welles had found the time to interview his witness.

"Is that his last name?" Abbie asked. "Okay, I only knew him as Jeremy. But he was looking for Joaninha too. Even asked for her by that name."

Brunelle cocked his head at Abbie. "Jeremy?" he repeated. Then, "Ms. Bishop, could you just go ahead and clarify which of those men you're talking about? The older man in the suit, or the younger man in the open-collared dress shirt?"

He could have just said, 'The white guy or the Asian guy?' but that seemed insensitive. And he had graduated that sensitivity class after all.

"The Asian guy," Abbie went ahead and said it. "Like I said, he told me his name was Jeremy. I didn't know his last name was Welles."

"It's not," Brunelle advised her. "It's Nguyen. Jeremy Nguyen. He's the defendant."

"Oh," Abbie said. Then she nodded. "Yeah, that makes sense now."

Welles stood up. "Your Honor, I'm sorry but I'm going to have to object again. This line of questioning has absolutely no relevance to the question before this jury."

"I disagree," Judge Tillerson replied. "Strongly. This door is open now, Mr. Welles. We're going to see where it leads. You may continue, Mr. Brunelle."

There was an old adage among trial attorneys: never ask a question you don't already know the answer to. And it was good advice, generally speaking. Know your case and make the witness admit to it. But sometimes things happen, and you can't fail to follow a path just because you don't know where it goes.

"Did Mr. Nguyen—Jeremy—tell you why he was looking for Joaninha?" Brunelle asked. Anything a witness said outside of court was hearsay and presumed inadmissible, unless it was the opposing party who said it. Anything Nguyen said could and would be used against him, whether it was to a cop, a friend, or Abbie Bishop.

"Not exactly," Abbie answered. "I mean he didn't come right out and say it, but he made sure I knew he'd heard she was looking to move some drugs from Brazil, and he was interested in helping her."

Welles jumped to his feet. "Objection, Your Honor! This is outrageous, simply outrageous. I can't even count the number of evidence rules this violates, let alone the Constitutional ramifications. Again, I'm sorry, Your Honor, but I have no choice but to demand a mistrial."

Brunelle smiled inside. Shouting 'Objection!' told the jury, 'Ouch.'

Shouting mistrial told them, 'I just lost.'

"It's a statement of a party-opponent," Brunelle responded. "Evidence Rule 801(d)(2)."

"Objection overruled," Tillerson said. Motion for mistrial denied. Proceed, Mr. Brunelle."

Welles huffed several times, but ultimately went ahead and sat down again as Brunelle continued. Of course, Brunelle didn't know where he was going; he just hoped he'd know when he got there.

"Did he say anything else?" he asked.

"He said he was finally going to 'get paid'." She made air quotes. "And no one was going to stand in his way."

And Brunelle had arrived at his destination. He was glad for it, but he also knew once they stepped onto the platform, he and Abbie would go their separate ways.

"Thank you, Ms. Bishop," he said. "No further questions."

Brunelle returned to his seat trying to suppress the spring in his step. Welles stood up, his own legs shaky. He didn't know where the Bishop Express was going either. But once a train jumped the tracks, the only way forward was down.

"You claim you spoke with my client?" he started.

"I didn't claim it," Abbie answered. "I said it."

"And you claim he was looking for someone named Joaninha," Welles continued, "which is a Portuguese martial arts nickname, who was only in the country for a short time, in order to execute some sort of drug transaction, but you don't really know the details. Is that right?"

Abbie thought for a moment. "Yup. That's right."

"How in the world would he know this woman, or her nickname, or that she was looking to sell drugs?"

"I have no idea," Abbie answered. "you'd have to ask her."

Welles smiled, knowing that would never happen.

"Except," Abbie volunteered, "she's in jail for shooting the lead detective on this case when he tried to talk to her."

Welles's smile disappeared, departing his face like a butterfly taking wing—an angry, frustrated butterfly with a law degree. That derailed train had just slid down the hill and burst into flames.

He had no choice but to cut his losses. "No further questions."

"Any redirect examination, Mr. Brunelle?" Judge Tillerson asked. "Or may this witness be excused?"

Brunelle stood up. "The witness may be excused, Your Honor."

"Any further rebuttal witnesses?" the judge asked.

Brunelle had intended on putting Montero on the stand. But he didn't need to. She would just repeat what Abbie had said. And Abbie had said it so much better than he could have ever hoped. "No, Your Honor. The State has no further witnesses."

Tillerson turned then and began explaining to the jury that this concludes the evidence portion of the trial, next will be jury instructions and then closing arguments. Brunelle had heard it a hundred times, at least. He didn't need to listen. Which was good because Meckle was in his ear.

"Oh my God, she was amazing," he gushed. "How did you find her?"

Brunelle thought for a moment. "I don't know." But he knew how he'd lost her.

But thanks to her, he wasn't going to lose the case.

CHAPTER 41

Welles grabbed Brunelle before he could leave the courtroom.

"That stunt will never hold up on appeal," he snarled. "Her testimony was full of inadmissible hearsay, base conjecture, and slanderous insinuation. And she never should have been allowed to testify in the first place. Tillerson may have given you the green light to violate my client's rights, but the Court of Appeals will send this back so fast, your precious Detective Chen will still be in the hospital for the next trial too."

"Murder Two," Brunelle answered. "With the firearm sentencing enhancement. You can argue for low end. But if it goes to the jury and they come back Murder One, I'm asking for the max."

Welles blinked at him. "Is that an offer?"

"It's the last offer," Brunelle responded. "And it expires as soon as we all leave the courtroom. He wants it, he takes it now. We pull Tillerson out of chambers; I amend the charge; and your guy pleads, right here, right now. It shaves a decade off his sentence."

Welles didn't reply. One thing about a person who talks all the time: it was really noticeable when he shut up. "I'll have to talk to my client."

"Of course," Brunelle said. "But hurry. The guards look ready to take him back to his cell. Give him some hope he'll get out of one before he's too old to care any more."

Welles nodded and went back to consult with Nguyen.

"Why did you offer that?" Meckle asked. "Ms. Bishop did great. The jury knows he's a drug dealer and they know that ladybug lady shot Detective Chen."

"He's not on trial for shooting Chen," Brunelle answered in a whisper. "He's on trial for shooting a competing drug dealer who had a gun in his hand too. Once that door closes and deliberations begin, there's no way to know what they're thinking, and there's no way to know what they'll do. I don't like it, and neither does Welles, which means it's probably the right thing to do. The best compromises are when no one is happy."

Carlisle walked up to them from her spot in the gallery. "What just happened? Did you offer him Murder Two?"

Brunelle nodded. "Yeah."

"Good call," Carlisle said. "He has to take it. After the way Abbie testified, his guy looks like a total dirtbag. 'No one is getting in the way of my payday' or whatever? Are you kidding me? God, I knew I liked her."

"Yeah, she's pretty awesome," Brunelle admitted.

"And single, right?" Carlisle teased. "I mean, you struck out. So, maybe I have a shot. You think she might be …?"

"I literally have no idea," Brunelle answered. "And I kinda don't care either. Knock yourself out."

"Okay, but if you keep pouting, you're not going to be invited to the wedding."

Unexpectedly, Judge Tillerson suddenly reentered the courtroom. Even the bailiff seemed taken off guard.

"Uh, all rise! Court is back in session, The Honorable Thomas Tillerson presiding."

Tillerson took the bench again and looked down at the attorneys before him. Carlisle slipped back to the gallery. Meckle sat down. Brunelle and Welles remained standing.

"I thought fifteen minutes would probably be enough time," the judge said. "Am I really going to have to bring this jury back tomorrow?"

Brunelle looked over to Welles. Welles looked back, then lowered his eyes and surrendered a confirmatory nod.

Brunelle looked back up at Judge Tillerson. "No, Your Honor. The defendant will be pleading guilty to an amended charge of murder in the second degree."

"And I assume no one is happy with this result?" the judge asked.

His question was met with shrugs and half-nods from the attorneys although no verbal confirmation.

"Good," Tillerson said. "Then that's probably justice."

EPILOGUE

Brunelle got a murder conviction.

Nguyen got twenty years.

Welles got a fat check and his name in the paper.

Chen got discharged.

Meckle got some experience.

And Abbie got away.

"One more," Brunelle told the bartender. He was at the bar right around the corner from his condo. He could have another.

"Whiskey, neat. Got it," the bartender replied and stepped away to pour the drink.

"Hey, stranger," came a voice over his shoulder.

He turned to see the voice's owner.

"Oh, hey," he said. "What are you doing in Seattle?"

"Long story," she said. "Buy a girl a drink?"

END

ABOUT THE AUTHOR

Stephen Penner is an attorney, author, and artist from Seattle.

In addition to the *David Brunelle Legal Thriller Series*, he also writes the *Talon Winter Legal Thrillers*, starring Tacoma criminal defense attorney Talon Winter, the *Maggie Devereaux Paranormal Mysteries*, recounting the exploits of an American graduate student in the magical Highlands of Scotland, and several stand-alone works.

For more information, please visit *www.stephenpenner.com*.